Jewels Are Her Vengeance

Terry Rajan

Cover design by Matthew Avery

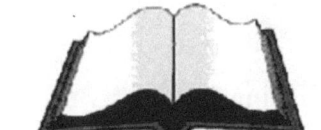

CCB Publishing
British Columbia, Canada

Jewels Are Her Vengeance

Copyright ©2008 by Terry Rajan
ISBN-13 978-1-926585-06-2
First Edition

Library and Archives Canada Cataloguing in Publication

Rajan, Terry
Jewels are her vengeance / written by Terry Rajan.
ISBN 978-1-926585-06-2
I. Title.
PS8635.A455J49 2008   C813'.6   C2008-906239-6

United States Copyright Office Registration # TXu 1-070-190

Publisher: CCB Publishing
             British Columbia, Canada
             www.ccbpublishing.com

Chapter 1

Thieves

It was September, the beginning of the rainy season in Seattle. Black clouds rolled over downtown, heralding the onslaught of torrential rain. Ice-cold shards pounded down to earth, plinking on car windshields and stained sidewalks. The midnight skyline became the perfect backdrop for this dazzling display of black sky and low thunder. No one could be seen walking the downtown streets that night. The emptiness was broken only by two dark figures hurrying down the wet and deserted streets—Tom, about thirty-eight years old, with a beer belly wearing dirty black clothes; and behind him, Dick, in his early fifties, tall, and somewhat greasy-looking. Their goal was the large, three-story glass building just a few blocks ahead. Lightning flashed, illuminating the towering Space Needle a couple of miles to the right. Both men were breathing heavily, slinking along the walls as they approached the glass building. They checked the streets for any unplanned observers—empty. The building was dark; the employees long since gone for the day. The only sounds were the patter of rain and the quiet wheezing of Tom catching his breath. A single spotlight shone above the side door discreetly shadowed, exposing anyone there to open with scrutiny. Dick snuffed out the wall lights near an entrance to the building with a spray of black paint. The area was immediately plunged into sudden darkness, which afforded the two men an increased amount of privacy. Tom relieved himself of the cumbersome backpack he had been toting and breathed a sigh of relief as the weight was lifted from his chubby shoulders.

Tom positioned a vacuum cup against the glass door near its base and stepped aside as Dick moved in, wielding a formidable looking steel rod. The rod was a nine-inch pipe with a "diamond wheel" on its tip, which Dick inserted into the middle of the vacuum cup. One circular cut and—luckily, it worked on the first try! A round pane of glass, about a foot and a half in diameter, became a new window. Tom released the pressure of the vacuum cup and the pane pulled free. He swore as he struggled to place the heavy slab of glass gently on the ground. Dick looked at him with amusement.

"There's a reason why I brought you, fatty. You can do all the heavy lifting."

Tom glared at Dick and leaned the glass against the wall and then plopped his bulk right down next to it, breathing heavily. Dick grinned—a hard, sneering grin—and moved closer to examine the hole in the door.

"Your fat ass won't fit through this hole. I'll go on ahead and disable the alarm and then let you in through the door."

Anger swept over Tom's normally jovial face. With a dark scowl, he told Dick, "Call me fat one more time, and I'll break your face."

Dick just laughed and pulled a black hood over his face. He slipped stealthily through the hole, twisting his slim, agile body easily into the building. He poked his head back out to give some final instructions to Tom, who was still sitting against the wall, looking quite disgruntled.

"You'll have to be cool. Don't panic and don't do anything stupid. I'm the one taking the big risks here, you know." Dick secured a radio receiver into his ear. Tom frowned even more.

"Are you sure you know what you're doing?

"Shut up! I did the freaking wiring here. I know every inch of this place. Just get your mask on and don't take it off—no matter what. There are cameras all over, and most of them work on motion sensors. Any movement and they've got you on film."

"Why didn't you cut the cameras too?" Tom asked in bewilderment.

Now it was Dick's turn to look angry. "I didn't do the wiring on the alarms, okay? I don't even know where the control cabinet is for the alarms. You just keep your mask on at all times and don't move around." Tom reluctantly nodded and donned his own mask and earpiece as Dick pulled his head back through the hole.

Dick's voice crackled through just seconds later. "Can you hear me?"

Tom replied loud and clear, "Yeah, yeah."

Dick winced and adjusted his receiver. "Not so freaking loud, stupid. Put the glass circle back and seal it up while I disable the alarm." Tom rolled his eyes and prepared for the struggle of putting back the round pane of glass. He grunted and strained as he lifted the glass into place, sweating profusely as he did. Once the glass was in place, Tom secured it with thick, clear tape. A loud crash from behind startled him out of his senses and he whined anxiously into the mouthpiece.

"Man, hurry up, I heard some noises!"

Dick cursed at him. "I'm trying to concentrate here. Just shut up and hold on!" Tom looked around to try and find the source of the noise that had startled him. He almost collapsed with relief when he realized that it was just a drunk stumbling around and overturning garbage cans in an alley across the street. A low metallic "clang" and a soft click sounded from the area of the door.

Dick's voice came through the radio, hurried and breathless.

"I killed the alarm. Open the door slowly and stay near the stairs. Don't smoke and don't make a sound. Tell me if you see anyone." Tom glanced around the deserted streets and quickly opened the door and let himself in.

"Okay, I'm in. Now make it quick. I'm scared and sweating my brains out over here." He stumbled over to the stairs and collapsed on the third step, rubbing his forehead through the mask to soak up some of the sweat. He took up a silent, weary vigil to make sure no one was watching their escapade.

Dick slowly perused the building's dimly-lit interior, noting the location of security cameras and exit routes. When he was satisfied with his basic knowledge of the layout of the bottom floor, he began climbing the stairs, again taking his time. He walked purposefully up to the third floor where there were rows of dark offices facing each other on both sides of a long hallway. The carpet was thick and plush, the walls artistically and tastefully decorated. Leaves of different plants reached through the blinds on the windows of the offices, brushing against the glass. Dick stopped in front of the second to the last door, a small smile creeping across his lips at the success of the first stage of what would be his grand triumph.

He pulled out a small steel instrument, similar to a tool a locksmith would use. Then he carefully inserted it, twisting the device into the door lock and within a minute the door was open. He slowly swung the door open and then closed it behind him, making sure it remained unlocked. He entered the room and paused—all was eerily still and quiet. The office belonged to a coin dealer, and it was definitely reflected by the posh appearance of the room. Rich mahogany wainscoting complemented the light green printed wallpaper above it and a soft leather office chair was neatly parked behind a large, dark brown desk. The carpet was thick and the shelves were decorated with plants and expensive-looking knickknacks. A small metal box sat in the corner. Dick's eyes lit on it, and it filled him with anticipation. That was it—the reason for the late-night break-in. In the opposite corner, unseen by Dick, was a small box with the time and date flashing on its screen. It was recording his every movement by a camera that was hidden in the ceiling. The camera watched silently as Dick picked the lock to the cabinet and opened it. Ah, so far so good. Dick breathed a sigh of relief realizing just how tense he was.

Now on the top of the stairs, Tom waited impatiently for Dick to finish. The silence was broken by gurgling sounds coming from his stomach and Tom sighed in discomfort. But he was prepared—he took a candy bar from his pocket and began to unwrap it, being careful not to drop it. He slowly peeled back the wrapper and took a bite of the thick chocolate and caramel treat.

Dick filled a duffel bag with the contents of the cabinet, working as silently as he possibly could even though his fingers had started to tremble. His heart pounded; his palms sweating profusely. He expected the alarm to go off at any moment; that would, at a moment's notice, cause armed guards to burst into the room. He worked faster, the fear of exposure spurring him on.

Tom tried to eat quickly, but the candy bar wouldn't fit inside the hole of his mask. He glanced around—hopefully Dick couldn't see—and lifted the mask above his mouth. There—he could eat now. But now sweat trickled down his forehead into his eyes. He looked around again, and then lifted the mask to wipe his forehead, exposing his face for just a few brief moments. That was all it took. On a TV monitor in a separate room, Tom was recorded as he happily munched on his snack.

Dick's voice came through suddenly: "See anyone? I'm done; I'm coming back right now."

Tom jumped and quickly replaced his mask. "No, no one's around."

Dick padded down the stairwell, a large duffel bag swinging from his shoulder and another in his hands. He handed Tom a bag. "Here, carry this. Don't drop it."

Tom stuffed the end of his candy bar in his mouth and grabbed the appropriate sack. As Dick and Tom retreated down the stairs, Tom left glistening boot-prints on the stairs. He looked in the bag and gasped, the candy bar falling from his mouth. Rows upon rows of shiny coins wrapped in thin plastic rolls basked in his admiring gaze.

Dick smiled. "Now you can afford that car." Both men slipped through the door and hurried away, their footsteps muffled by the splashing rain. The door swung slowly shut.

Chapter 2

Ideas Dawning

The next day, the early morning sun slowly crept up, chasing away the shadows on a high-rise apartment building. The structure was modern, chic, and well out of the price range of the average working person. The luxury penthouses occupied the top two floors and it was in the most extravagant one that Diane Taylor resided. Twenty-eight years old, in the prime of life, and beautiful—Diane was the woman that other women envied, the all-American beauty that dated the quarterback in high school and was the top of her class in her college years. Her thick dark brown hair was professionally highlighted and styled and her complexion was a perfect peaches-and-cream. Her eyes were a rich brown and her skin lightly bronzed by the sun. She looked perfectly at home in the lush suite that boasted rich fabrics and exquisite lighting. The soft rosy hue of the walls and the dark wood accents added to the wealthy aura of the loft.

Diane opened her walk-in closet, revealing racks of designer labels and expensive fabrics. In one corner, a small iron safe sat unobtrusively on a low shelf. Diane chose a pair of slim black heels, sensible only in the world of fashion and turned back into her bedroom. The wall opposite her bed was entirely composed of glass and showcased a magnificent view of the city from 32 stories up. From here, she watched the bustle of city life by day and the glittering of city life by night. Diane pushed a small button by her bed and automatic curtains closed, shielding her from any unwanted eyes. Her bed was plush, a king-size sleigh-bed with a soft down comforter and fluffy pillows. A thick rug complemented the soft color of the walls and added a striking element to the sterile white carpet. A fireplace sat quiet and dark in the corner opposite her bed. On the TV above the mantel, an enthusiastic woman's voice finished extolling the virtues of a certain brand of detergent as the news resumed.

"Good morning, Seattle!" A fresh-faced anchor woman exclaimed robustly, smiling cheerfully into the camera. "Our top story today involves a serious theft that occurred downtown between one and two o'clock this morning. Some rare coins were stolen from the Wynn Center. These coins were owned by a collector who was in town for a numismatics convention."

Diane sat on the edge of her bed and watched with undivided attention as she paused before slipping on her shoes.

The anchor woman continued, glancing down at her notes with a more serious expression on her face. "For those of you who are wondering what numismatics is, it is the study and collection of coins, medals, and paper money. Veronica Walsh is live at the scene. Veronica?" The scene cut to an older woman gripping a microphone, the Wynn Center a backdrop to the scene. The reporter, graying hair wildly drifting around her face, jockeyed for a spot in front of yellow police tape that was cordoning off the doorway where the thieves had broken in.

"The thieves gained entrance here"—she pointed to the glass door—"by removing a section of glass. They disabled the alarm system, and then stole away with the coin collection. I was lucky enough to find Detective Dave Merko at the scene to give us more information." The camera cut to a younger man talking intensely into a cell phone that seemed glued to his ear. He was about 30 years old, and could easily be mistaken for a Calvin Klein model rather than a detective. His dark hair was cut close to his head and his eyes a bright green. His eyelashes were a length that most women would kill for and he had just enough stubble on his cheeks to be rugged and not disheveled. He shot the camera a dark glance and held up his hand toward it, indicating his extreme disinterest in sharing any details. The reporter still moved in, however, her face alight with eagerness for a chance to distinguish herself.

"Detective, can you tell us a little bit about the robbery?"

Merko just waved her off, listening intently to the squawking voice in his ear. He turned away from the camera and pressed his free hand to his other ear in order to hear better. But Veronica Walsh was persistent—she motioned the cameraman to follow her as she circled around. Merko was closing the phone, his conversation finished.

"Is it true you think it was a professional job?" Veronica asked forcefully, thrusting the microphone into Merko's face.

The detective's face became resigned and he ran his hand over his cropped hair before beginning. "It was a burglary. That's all I can tell you now." His voice was calm but authoritative, belying his extensive experience with the press. Veronica looked rather disappointed, but pasted her bright smile back on as she made eye contact with the camera.

"For all you folks who just tuned in, we're broadcasting live from the Wynn Center in downtown Seattle, where there has been a theft of some valuable coins." The camera panned over a few inches to record a police photographer taking pictures of the scene.

Merko relented from his reticence and continued. "We've confirmed that this was done by professionals. The cut patterns on the glass indicate first-hand knowledge of the art. The surveillance footage shows two masked men in and out in 40 minutes."

As he spoke, the camera zoomed in on the stairwell just inside the door where a forensics technician lifted a footprint off a step using white paper gauze. Detective Merko seemed to realize where the camera was filming and he gestured toward the door, explaining as he did so.

"We have some leads. We have clear footprints, which gives us a definite tread pattern and shoe size. It's too early to divulge any other details."

Diane straightening from her sitting position and took several experimental steps on her thin heels before checking her reflection in the mirror, watching the news report reflecting from the glass as she took a second glance.

Merko fidgeted awkwardly as if he wanted to finish the conversation. "According to the owner of the coins, his collection alone is worth several hundred thousand dollars."

Diane turned away from the mirror and went to the door, listening to the rest of the report as she adjusted her suit jacket over her shapely hips.

Veronica put her two cents in quickly, wanting more face-time with the camera. "Many of our viewers may find it hard to believe that someone would pay a decade's worth of wages for a few coins."

Diane tapped her fingernails impatiently against the wall next to a framed photo, anxious for the report to finish so she could get to work. While she waited, she studied the picture. In the photograph, a group of about fifty people in business attire stood smiling and waving in front of her apartment building. Large white letters on the front of the building informed any picture-viewer that this place housed the elite business offices of The Rittman Developers. A man in his early 50's stood in front of the group, his arms outstretched and a wide smile that said, 'Look what I did! See how great it is!' Diane paced back to the TV and reached to shut it off right as Merko wrapped up the morning's segment of the coin theft.

"Well, from my experience, if somebody wants something bad enough—then no price is too high."

Diane froze mid-reach, staring at the screen.

Chapter 3

Paul Rittman Developer

A Porsche sports car whizzed by a construction site, driven by the man proudly situated in the forefront of the Rittman Developers' picture. Paul Rittman in early fifties was as healthy and robust as he had been at 35. He glanced through the wire mesh fence that separated him from the working class. Several workers were standing around, chatting on their cell phones or playing a game of soccer with a beat-up old ball. Paul picked up his cell phone and hit #7—speed-dialing his building project manager.

"John, I just passed the job site. Are you on schedule?"

A cheerful voice crackled through Paul's earpiece, making him wince. "Paul! I'm happy to tell you that we are a week ahead of schedule!"

Paul's mouth tightened and he accelerated through a yellow light. "Great. You know what would make me happy? Having the men I pay to work actually doing their jobs when I drive by."

There was a quick moment of silence on the other end and then: "Paul, I didn't know—they usually are. It's their break time."

Paul hung up. The mesh fence ended and a row of pretty little shops became the new scenery. He screeched into a parking spot in front of a flower shop and hopped out with a beep from the automatic locks. After a few minutes he reappeared, holding a bouquet of exotic-looking flowers in one hand and in his briefcase in the other. A click of the lock, a rev of the powerful engine, and Paul was off again, zipping aggressively through traffic until he reached a large office building. He strode under the large sign proclaiming this grand 32-story building to be Rittman Developers and into the main lobby, which housed the office area. The rest of the 31 floors were homes to luxurious apartments where only the very wealthy resided. Paul approached the massive reception desk, his swagger indicating that he did, in fact, own the place. An uptight-looking secretary whose name badge read *Linda* looked up as he drew near.

"Good morning, Mr. Rittman."

Paul nodded without slowing his pace. "Good morning." As he rounded the corner, Linda called hurriedly after him.

"I'll bring you your coffee, sir!"

"Thank you, Linda." Paul's words echoed around the corner. The lobby was comprised of marble floors and pillars, dark wood furnishings, and forest green walls. Everything was state-of-the-art and completely up-to-date. The click of stiletto heels on the marble mingled with the loud buzz of busy voices and the beep of computers. Soaring glass panels bathed the lobby with soft natural light, keeping the area from looking cold and corporate.

Paul headed directly for the door labeled *Diane Taylor, Chief Architect* and knocked loudly.

"Come in!'

Paul entered, flashing that smile that had brought him millions along with a confident aura radiating about him. Diane barely glanced up from her work—just enough to see who it was. Paul held out the flowers—Diane lifted her eyes briefly but returned to her work again. It was a game they played—who would look first, who would make the connection of eyes and emotions. Paul began singing quietly.

"Happy Birthday to you, Happy Birthday to you…" Diane was losing the game, struggling valiantly to keep her attention on her desk as a small smile threatened to appear. "Happy Birthday, dear Diane…" Diane gave up and made eye contact as she accepted the bouquet. Paul quickly glanced over his shoulder and then leaned close to kiss her on the cheek, "Happy Birthday."

Diane buried her flushing cheeks in the welcoming faces of the flowers and deeply breathed in the cool scent. "You're coming tonight?" She asked, almost shyly.

Paul smiled enigmatically. "Maybe." He winked and nodded toward the door, indicating the possibility of listening ears. "Got to go," he mouthed silently, heading toward the door. He blew her a kiss and left just as quickly as he had come in. Diane was smiling sincerely now, her face looking younger than her 28 years. She drank in the sweet fragrance of the flowers as she rummaged through the shelves of the nearby credenza for a vase. The flowers were then skillfully arranged in the crystal vase—another gift from Paul—giving the flowers an extended drink of water. Diane cast about as to where to put the vase that was now overflowing with soft petals and lush greenery and settled on the corner of her desk as the perfect spot. She went back to work with a quiet smile and a fierce determination to finish her work as quickly as possible.

Chapter 4

Love in Danger

In Diane's living room, the disinterested clock face read 6:00 PM. The sun was setting, sending golden rays slanting across the carpet. The flowers that Diane had caressed so tenderly earlier were on the floor, the vase not bothering to restrain the life-giving water anymore. Diane was on her back on the table, Paul above her. The first fire of passion had settled into a flicker and the two kissed with lingering, deep kisses in between breaks in their low, throaty conversation. Paul broke off another kiss and fingered the large diamond necklace around Diane's neck.

"You like your birthday present?"

Diane smiled playfully. "Yes. Thank you. And…the necklace isn't so bad either."

Paul laughed and pulled her into his arms. He lowered his head and kissed her again, more fervently this time. The fire began to reignite and the couple moved quickly into the bedroom, pulling the door shut behind them. After a few hours, Diane came back into the living room in just her robe, her hair disheveled and her eyes bright. She gathered the flowers into a haphazard bunch and put them back into the vase. Paul leaned against the doorjamb, buttoning his shirt slowly and watching her move about. She refilled the vase with water and put the flowers back on the table, bashfully keeping her eyes downcast on her tasks. For an awkward few seconds, no one spoke. Then they both spoke at once, Diane raising her eyes to Paul's face and Paul looking away guiltily.

"Are you staying tonight?"

"I should get going." Paul looked back up at Diane, his face softening. "Maybe after this weekend. Greg is coming home from the university for a visit tomorrow, so tonight's not a good time."

Diane shrugged. "I understand." There was a short pause, and then Diane continued, quietly, her voice regretful." I'm 29 today. Next year I'll be 30. I'm not young anymore." She met his eyes defiantly, anger sparking for the first time in their relationship. "Actually, you know what? I don't understand. We've been seeing each other for six years. There have been six birthdays, and six expensive gifts. But what you don't see is that I don't care about the necklaces or the vases or the apartment or any of it! All I really want from you is five simple words."

Paul answered just as his cell phone began ringing in his jacket pocket. "What five words?"

"You told me three years ago that you would move in with me." Diane clenched and unclenched her fists, her face lined with anger and sorrow. Paul's cell phone rang again. He shot her a helpless look and reached for it.

"Hello, dear. Yes, yes...Not a problem. Yes—I'll pick those up...Yes..." Paul looked at Diane. The last sentence Paul said to his wife but meant for Diane only. "I love you." Paul hung up and continued gazing at Diane. She dropped her gaze, fingering the necklace nervously. Paul sighed and shrugged the cell phone into his jacket.

"Do you want me to put the necklace in the safe for you?" Paul asked gently. Diane smiled weakly and nodded, struggling with the clasp. Paul approached and reached behind her neck, unhooking the necklace for her. "I know I promised a lot—maybe more than I

16

should have. But six years ago, the kids were younger and I just thought that we could work something out once they were older. But now with Greg halfway through college and Christina getting married to the senator's son---they need their mother and me together." Paul slid his hands down Diane's arms and intertwined his fingers with hers. "My marriage is a formality, but it's also an asset. Stability in the home equals stability in the workplace. I could lose a lot more than my wife and the respect of my children if I leave them now."

Diane clung to his hands. "How much am I worth to you?" She asked soberly.

Paul dangled the necklace. "A lot more than this." He smiled reassuringly and Diane released her grip on his hand. Paul, feeling guilty, added quickly, "I'll find somewhere to take you next week to make it up to you, okay?" Diane nodded, her face resigned, and moved away from him. Paul left her to go into the bedroom and, in view of the living room where Diane stood, opened the safe and placed the necklace in a black box that was brimming with valuable gems. The rest of the safe was filled with neatly stacked bundles of cash. Paul retrieved one of the bundles and slipped it into his pocket and then placed the jewel box back on the bottom of the safe. A few quick turns of the lock, and he straightened from his crouched position. Diane, her eyes brightening as she held back tears, watched him in silence as he hurriedly blew her a kiss and walked out the door. She reached into a low, inconspicuous cupboard and pulled out a bottle of Scotch.

Chapter 5

A Night Alone

Diane lay back on the bed pillows, taking a long pull of the amber bottle in her hand. Her normally cheerful attitude had fallen into a depressive slump, her shoulders low and her spirits even lower. She took another swig from the bottle and placed it clumsily back on the bedside table, the contents sloshing around in the bottom. Diane reached for the small book on the bed beside her—her diary with her name embossed in gold on the front cover. She had filled the pages in this diary when she was in college—young and impressionable, ambitious, eager to make her mark on the world. She was passionate about architecture, thirsty for knowledge and moral in character. While her friends partied their careers away, she studied and crammed and excelled.

Diane flipped through the pages, reading her entries that were full of dreams for the future, opinions about politics, and struggles in relationships. She wanted to be the architect designing individual luxury homes—"I want to help people fulfill their dreams," the informed voter—"The president is crazy!" and the perfect wife and mother—"I want to find the love of my life soon!" Diane blinked back tears as she thought about where she had come since those nine short years; she was designing corporate structures—she was bored to death, she didn't even know who was running for president—John? Jim?—and she was involved in an affair with a married man. She reached for the bottle again, letting the burning liquid soothe her troubled conscience with the salve that had patched up so many of her wounds before. She turned the page and saw the list that she had jotted down so long ago.

"MY GOALS," the title read. Diane laughed cynically to herself. She already knew what was going to be on that list. Better character traits than she had developed, higher life ambitions than she had attained, and a painful reminder of what she hadn't done with her life. Sure enough, at the bottom of the list, a sentence in bold capitals jumped out at her: "**WEALTH AND MARRIAGE BEFORE I TURN 30**." She had certainly attained the wealth, but the loneliness inside her made her want to scream. A sexual fling with a married man just couldn't compare with a stable, love-filled life with a committed man. As much as she enjoyed Paul's company, she knew she was missing out on something much better.

The TV now blared an infomercial. An effeminate man, with lots of flashy jewelry and greasy hair, appeared on the screen, grinning toothily.

"Are you well on your way to attaining your life's goals? Or did you just cross another wish off your list of dreams?" The man's face drooped theatrically as he tried to curb his fake enthusiasm. "Sadly, ever-increasing majorities of you are living the latter." The cheesy over-excited tone returned in full force. "But it doesn't have to be that way!"

"Easy for you to say, pal!" Diane cried drunkenly at the screen. "You're not having an affair with a married man!"

The host swished over to a chalkboard, his hips swaying in a very feminine way. "So, let's do what we talked about earlier. Let's write down our goals. Just grab a pen and paper to jot them down or just say them out loud to yourself. Let's look at some common goals for the average person." In a bold, scrawling hand, the host wrote "Wealth" across the top of the board. "For a lot of people, wealth is their top priority in life. It's their link to a feeling of security, which, in turn, makes them comfortable and confident enough to pursue and attain their other goals."

"You want my list?" Diane shouted angrily at the television set. The host is drowned out by her yelling. "Wealth, marriage, happiness! All those before my next birthday!" She crumpled into the covers, weeping violently. Tears dripped off her nose, into her ears, soaking her pillows.

The infomercial host was smiling cheerfully again. "If you order my 30-day program, I will teach you how to create attainable goals, manifest them, and then live them."

Diane clicked off the TV abruptly. She drained the bottle and took up the discourse with herself again. "Mr. Paul Rittman, you taught me that I shouldn't let anything stand in my way. Set a goal and attain it! That's what you told me. Well, I'm going to do it. I will be wealthy and married before my next birthday. You just watch me!" Diane stumbled out onto her balcony where the fresh breeze caressed her flushed cheeks. She stood on a deck chair drunkenly and cried her misery to the world. "Set a goal and attain it!" The chair wobbled dangerously and she tripped on the slats. She balanced precariously for a second and then staggered back inside.

It was hopeless. Her life was worth nothing. She was worth nothing. Despair came in great, gulping sobs as she curled up on her giant bed. Alone, and unloved.

Diane fell asleep, mumbling slowly to herself. "My goals….I will. I will…"

Chapter 6

Two Months Later

Diane hummed a nondescript tune under her breath as she made her way into the apartment lobby. This wasn't the Diane of two months ago. No, this Diane was confident, hopeful, and more than ready to get on with her life. She thought wryly that although she was ready for a different phase in her life, she was still working on the weekends—something she hadn't quite been able to stop doing. She was still lonely sometimes; Paul hadn't been over near as often as she would have hoped. But life was going to be better now—Diane was determined to make it that way. She fit her key into her mailbox slot and opened it with some trepidation. No bad news, and no bills; those were the things she hated to see the most. But she was lucky this time. She ruffled through the pile that turned out to be mostly junk mail except for a personally addressed envelope. Ah, Christina Rittman was getting married. And, ironically, Diane was invited to the shower.

The door blew open jingly and Diane couldn't help but smile when she saw who had come in. Chandra, the gorgeous East Indian woman who lived just one floor below Diane, adjusted her Prada purse over a shoulder as she clacked across the marble floor. She was surprisingly funny and down-to-earth—qualities that had endeared her to Diane as soon as they met. Chandra looked askance at Diane's business attire.

"Work on a weekend—the ultimate fashion accessory." She remarked sarcastically. Diane just laughed. Chandra shrugged and opened her own mailbox—empty. "Hm, my invitation to dinner at the White House must still be on the way." Diane felt even better than she had been feeling earlier. Nothing like a good dose of Chandra to brighten one's day! She followed the younger woman to the elevator, hoping to get a chance to talk a little more. She shouldn't have worried about that. Chandra chattered on and on about last night's party, the social gathering, the other weekend, drama between her friends, a new relationship she was trying to get on its feet, and her latest problems with her mother.

Suddenly, a wave of loneliness hit Diane and she wished she hadn't gotten on the elevator. Hearing all the stories of all the friends and family in Chandra's life just highlighted the fact that she was alone. She tried to bring back some of the good feelings of earlier and failed. Then she looked down at the mail in her hand. Sitting on the top was that shower invitation. She already knew she was going to be there by herself. She didn't know anyone who would go with her, except....Diane decided to take a chance.

"Hey, Chandra, want to be my date week after next?"

Chandra looked over with a sparkle in her eye. "Prince Charming's ball?"

Diane laughed a little. "I wish. It's a bridal shower, actually. For my boss's daughter. I sort of have to go. His wife is boring, but the door prizes will make it totally worth it." The elevator dinged their arrival to Chandra's floor.

Chandra nodded agreeably. "Okay, I'm there. Call me later with the details." Diane agreed quickly before she could change her mind. Chandra disappeared from sight as the elevator door closed again. Diane looked down at the invitation again, and smiled.

Diane pursed her lips in thought as she carefully penciled in another angle. She was sitting cross-legged on the floor in front of the coffee table where she had laid out numerous papers and designs. The TV was on fairly low, and she glanced up occasionally to catch the biggest news. The picture of the newsroom with its well-dressed newscasters switched over to an on-scene female reporter, who didn't seem to mind interviewing the handsome detective from a couple of months ago. Diane didn't mind looking at him either, and turned up the volume.

"How did you find the thieves?" The middle-aged reporter was close to the bounds of professional behavior as she inched closer, smiling like a Cheshire cat all the while.

Detective Dave Merko smiled a little, the triumph of his victory still clear in his excited eyes. "One of the thieves left a clear shoe print on the ground floor on the stairs and the other left one on the third floor level. The lookout guy left the ones on the ground floor and on the stairs. Thankfully for us, it was a rainy day, so the prints were clear. The building's motion sensor of the security cameras recorded all the details that we needed to identify the thieves."

"One question that I think the general public might have is this: If the evidence needed to identify the criminals were so easy to record and use, then why did it take almost two months to find the thieves?"

Merko looked straight into the camera, his confidence exuding warmth and familiarity. Diane felt more comfortable just looking at him on the screen. "Analyzing the evidence and identifying and catching criminals takes time. We have to be 100 percent sure that we've got the right person before we make a move. Too many innocent people have paid for crimes that they didn't commit."

The reporter smiled in anticipation of the rise in ratings that would come from the answer to her next question. "So are you 100 percent sure you've got the right men?"

"Yes, ma'am, we're 100 percent sure."

Diane smiled, saying to herself, "Those guys didn't plan well enough. You have to plan well to succeed; just like planning a building and building with quality , within the budgeted cost and completing the project on time."

Chapter 7

The Game Starts

In downtown Seattle, the clock of an old cathedral chimed out the time: 9:00 pm. The streets surrounding the church were rough, full of gangs and bad blood. The neighborhood was notorious for its history of violence and poverty, evidenced by graffiti-covered walls and the constant wail of sirens coming and going. The streetlights were dim, elongating shadows and shrouding dark alleys in wariness. This was Caficio's home, his place of origin. He had grown up in a small, crowded house just two blocks from where he now stood, at a street corner across from the soaring cathedral. He was small, Hispanic, and had a hardness in his dark eyes that belied his years on the streets. An aunt and her three older sons, all of whom belonged to a tough street gang, also occupied the home he had lived in. Caficio's mother had worked long hours with his aunt at a local store and his cousins had been left the task of watching out for him. That meant that he tagged along as they vandalized, destroyed, and threatened the area. He had learned from a young age—he was 10 when they moved in— how to look out for himself. He had stolen his first item at 10, been beat up numerous times at 11, and beaten someone up for the first time at 12. By 15, he was a regular drug dealer for several men and women and had been involved in multiple armed robberies.

Now in his late 20's, the lack of childhood showed clearly in the lines of his face and in his dealings with others. His thin body was covered in tattoos—one for each year he had survived. His dark hair was kept short and his clothing dark and loose fitting. He had dealt in petty deals long enough, however. He was looking for a big job, something that would haul in a lot of cash. And now he had a lead; he was just waiting for the call.

Caficio's cell phone beeped, a red light flashing to alert him of an incoming call. "Talk to me."

"Caficio?" A woman's voice spoke quietly, hesitantly.

"Yeah. Who's this?"

"I have a job, if you're interested."

Caficio tightened his grip on the small silver phone in anticipation. "Who are you?"

"I don't know you and you don't know me. Let's just keep it that way." The woman hesitated. "But, if you really need a name, call me…Medea. Think it over. I'll call you back tomorrow."

Caficio hurried to cut her off before she hung up. "Wait! I don't need to think about it. What service would you like me to provide?" A truck barreled past, its muffler roaring and bass thumping as Caficio pressed the phone closer to his ear. A satisfied look came over his face as the voice on the other end filled him in. "I can do that, except I want the pay to be in cash and I want it worth my time."

"You will be paid one thousand dollars."

Caficio digested this bit of information and decided to accept. "Okay. I'll do it, exactly like you said."

"Good. I'll be in touch." The phone went silent and then the dial tone buzzed in his ear. Caficio tucked the phone back into his pocket and lit a cigarette, smiling craftily.

The next day Diane sat alone in her office, examining some papers that were strewn around her desk. There was a slight knock at the door, and Paul entered, shutting the door softly behind him.

"Diane, I just…uh…I really appreciate your patience with me lately, and to show you my…my appreciation…well…" Diane looked up for the first time and saw Paul extending an envelope toward her. She watched him questioningly as she took the envelope and slid the contents into her hand.

"'Carmen' at the Opera House? That's the hottest show in town! How did you get these?" Diane couldn't help her excitement. Paul looked substantially more at ease now and perched on the edge of her desk, a pleased smile crossing his features.

"I begged, borrowed, and stole. All for you honey."

Diane gave him a conspiratorial smile. "That's right. I know your connections."

Paul returned the grin and sifted through some of the papers on her desk. "What are you working on?" He leaned closer to the papers, and Diane moved them away quickly.

"I'm just tidying up the details on the Oahu project. I'm making sure all the facts are shown." She strategically steered Paul away from the desk.

"Well, don't work too late. Take some rest and learn to relax. Christina can't wait to see you this weekend. Accepting Lisa's invitation to the shower definitely shows that the class I've tried to instill in you has taken hold."

Diane looked up with a mischievous grin. "And it looks good for you. I mean, if we were having an affair, then why would I, in my right mind, go to your house and cozy up to your family and friends?"

Paul missed the humor sparkling in her eyes and gave her a

surprised look. "It's not like that. I'd let the whole world know about us if things were different."

Diane patted his hand rather maternally. "Paul, relax. I was just teasing."

Paul looked relieved, pretending to wipe imaginary sweat from his brow. "Yeah, I knew that." He bent over and kissed her warmly. "I'll see you later." Diane watched him go and then shredded the copies of a building's security alarm system. The paper descended into the blades, writhing and contorting as they met their death…

The evening was purple and gold, hazy with strange warmth in the air for being November in western Washington. A thick bank of clouds lay far away on the horizon, promising the return of its trademark Seattle rain. In the apartment lobby, a young, skinny guard lounged at the security station, half-heartedly keeping an eye on the multiple screens. A movement on one of the screens caught his attention, and he quickly snapped into an alert pose as he waited for the elevator doors to open. He wasn't disappointed, although the view of Diane in person was far more stimulating than the image on the black and white screen. Diane wore a stunning black dress that exposed her cleavage and dipped dangerously low in the back. The thin straps looked as if they would slide off at any moment and the hemline swished tantalizingly around her shapely thighs. His breath labored as Diane approached, smiling and swaying her hips. She set the gift bag she was carrying on the counter and looked him up and down.

"Why, Trevor, that uniform is looking a little tight on you. Have you been working out?"

Trevor flushed nervously, and stammered out his answer. "A little. You gotta stay in shape for the job, you know."

"Then I'm sure you'll be able to do a little something for me."

Diane leaned closer, tracing a dainty finger across Trevor's badge.

Trevor tried manfully not to look at Diane's dress and failed miserably. "Uh, j-just name it and I'll, um, do it."

"Good. I have to run to the ladies' room. I'm expecting Chandra to meet me here at the lobby any minute; could you tell Chandra where I am when she gets here?"

"Yes, ma'am." Trevor beamed at her, clearly proud to be able to help her out.

"Thanks, Trevor."

Trevor started to walk to the front of the lobby to watch for Chandra.

Diane sauntered toward the ladies' room until she was out of the guard's sight. She then casually returned close to the desk where Trevor still didn't notice her. A series of monitors showing different views of hallways, corridors, and sidewalks sat behind the desk. A TV positioned next to the monitors, silently showing the news. A single camera swept the lobby area, blinking a piercing red light.

A horn honks outside. Chandra must have gone out a different way. Diane strode cheerfully to the front of the lobby. "That's my ride. Thanks again, Trevor." Diane slid into the creamy leather seat in Chandra's luxurious BMW. Chandra looked at Diane and raised her eyebrows in surprise.

"Look at you! You're dressed to kill."

Diane smiled. "Not quite."

They arrived at Paul Rittman's mansion, both not quite able to suppress their awe. The house was, to put it lightly, magnificent. Tall and white was the only way to describe it. Lights and ivy and pillars adorned the outside and the inside exuded warmth and noise. The doorman nodded politely when he opened the door to them and helped Chandra off with her coat. When Diane's outfit was revealed, he paused noticeably, his eyes flickering to her dress and then quickly away. Diane spotted Lisa Rittman approaching and quickly put on a friendly smile. The doorman remembered his duties and left quietly to hang up the coats.

Lisa was in her middle 50's but looked a little older. She was above average build and had a charming personality. "My husband said you might not come." Lisa greeted her with a warm hug and a genuine smile. "I asked him, 'Your chief architect not coming to our daughter's bridal party?' Then I told him, 'You wait and see. She'll come.' And here you are."

Diane felt her nerves tense and she replied shortly. "Well, it sounds like Paul underestimates me more than you do." Lisa lost some of her warmth and her smile wavered as she realized the hidden meaning in Diane's words. The two women regarded each other for several beats and then Chandra broke the uneasy tension.

"Hi, I'm Chandra. I hope it's all right that I came." She stuck her hand out for Lisa to shake. Lisa regained her composure and graciously shook Chandra's hand.

"You are more than welcome. You live in the same complex as Diane, correct?"

"Yes, I do. You have a good memory, Mrs. Rittman."

Lisa laughed a little. "Oh, please call me Lisa. We don't stand on formality around here."

"So where's the bride?" Diane interrupted.

"Oh, they're at the pool area. Shall we join them?" Lisa gestured toward the spacious patio where the guests were milling around. The three walked out to the patio—a landscaper's and architect's dream. The backyard would have been right at home in a palace. Diane marveled at the intricacy of the landscaping and the beauty of the plants. Champagne flowed freely, as did the chatter and the caviar. A live band added pleasant background noise to the hubbub of the women in attendance. Diane and Chandra found a comfortable spot to sit and watch as Christina opened her gifts, looking exactly as a future senator's wife ought to look.

Paul stood in a shadowed entryway, wine in hand, and watched Diane intently. He caught her eye and motioned her discreetly to come in his direction. Diane glanced around, and then silently acquiesced by getting up and moving toward him as he approached. She smiled as they came within earshot.

"Hey, handsome."

Paul frowned and looked around to make sure no one was watching. He peeked dubiously at her dress. "Do you really think that dress is appropriate?"

Diane cast a flirtatious glance upwards. "Perfectly appropriate. The doorman and the waiters like it." She pouted playfully.

Paul couldn't stop the corners of his mouth from lifting or his eyes from lingering on her youthful form. "I thought the idea was to blend."

Diane moved closer. "We could blend right here." Paul began to reply and then noticed Senator Thomas approaching. He pulled away from Diane and turned toward the senator. Thomas was tall, distinguished, and powerful in both political and business circles. He held a tennis racket and eyed Diane suspiciously as he neared.

"I'm going to be late for my match." He told Paul, looking him straight in the eye. Paul had the grace to look a little embarrassed.

"This is Christina's future father-in-law, Senator Thomas. Ken, this is Diane Taylor, one of my very talented architects. She is currently heading up the construction of a luxury hotel in Hawaii."

The lines of wariness on Thomas's face were quickly replaced by a suave leer. He bent over her hand elegantly. "My pleasure, Miss Taylor. Brains and beauty—a rare combination." He saluted Paul with his racket and turned to leave, casting a last glance at Diane's dress as he left. Paul again began to speak, but Christina interrupted him from across the room.

"Look, Daddy! Tickets to 'Carmen'!"

Paul shot Diane a disapproving glare and then joined his daughter and wife on the small couch where Christina was opening her presents. He slipped an arm around Christina's shoulders and kissed Lisa softly on the lips. A camera flashes, searing the image onto the film—picture perfect.

Chapter 8

Robbed

As the party swung gaily at the Rittman's luxurious home, all was quiet in the apartment lobby. The night shift security guard relieving Trevor of his duties unloaded a knapsack full of books, puzzles, and snacks, preparing himself for the long night ahead. The volume blared noisily as he turned on the TV to a local sports station. All the monitors, recording empty halls and deserted stairwells, sat behind him against the wall. The clock on the wall ticked off the seconds until the large hand reached the six, making it 10:30 PM on the dot. A shadow flashed across a monitor—the security guard, who was now watching a comedy show, laughed at a joke and didn't turn around. The shadow—a person, moving quickly and stealthily—opened an outside emergency door and entered the building.

At the mansion, Diane downed yet another glass of brandy and joined in the dancing, laughing with abandon as her usually keen faculties were quickly dulled by the effects of the alcohol. She wasn't alone, however. Women from 25-55, dresses sparkling and eyes shining, were swimming in a ocean of tipsiness, whirling and plunging and talking in loud, slurred voices. A small group of women were talking in a corner, unbridled laughter punctuating their conversation and another two women were passed out on the couch. Someone turned up the music and the lights and feet kept rhythm as the party grew louder and faster.

The clock showed 11:15 pm. The same monitor showed the dim figure exiting the same door he came in. But this time, the alarm was triggered. The guard jerked to alertness and spun around in his chair just in time to see the person sneaking away from the door, quickly disappearing into the shadows of the street. The guard grabbed for the phone and dialed 911, quickly explaining the problem. The intruder ran for it, the monitor immediately losing the visual. The guard waited at the front entrance until several squad cars pulled up, lights flashing across the street and reflecting in the glass panes of the building. Two middle-aged officers pulled the guard into the lobby and began questioning him.

"Did you see the person?"

"Only on the monitor, officer, just when he was coming out of the door." The security guard wrung his hands, clearly nervous about being interrogated by the police.

"Where does the door lead to?" The older of the two officers had a pen and notepad ready, watching the guard carefully for any signs of overly suspicious actions or answers.

The guard pointed toward the stairs. "The penthouse floor."

"Could anyone still be in the building?"

"I checked the monitors of all the floors, and there's no sign of movement."

The officer gestured to two other policemen standing near by. "Check all the floors for any sign of damage." They nodded respectfully and headed off to do their duty by way of the emergency stairwell. They didn't find any damage until they reached the penthouse floor. The flashlight illuminated a hole cut in the glass door.

"Hey, Jerry, tell me if this looks familiar."

The other officer came over to inspect the finding. "Looks like the scene at the Wynn Center with the coin robbery."

"That's what I thought, too. But we've got those guys behind bars." Martin shrugged. "Let's go tell the chief what we found." The two men jogged back down the stairs and reported their discovery to the officer in charge.

"Who lives in the penthouse?" He asked the guard, who was listening eagerly for any news.

"A Miss Diane Taylor."

"Do you know where she is?"

"The other guard on duty before me said that she left the building around six—dressed up, like for a party."

"Do you know what time she will be back"?

"No sir, no idea"

The officer glanced at his watch. "It's midnight, she should be back soon. We'll wait."

Chapter 9

Surprises

Diane gasped audibly when she saw what seemed like an army of black and white police cars in front of the apartment building. Chandra swore.

"What happened?" Diane asked in shock. "I wonder if someone was murdered."

"I hope not." Chandra replied grimly. "Here comes a cop. Hopefully he'll tell us what's going on." Diane rolled down the passenger window as the officer approached. He glanced inside the car; taking in the women's flushed cheeks and rumpled dresses.

"Do you live here?"

"Yes, we both do. What happened?" Diane gripped her purse in her hands.

"Looks like a burglary. What floor do you live on?"

Chandra chimed in first. "I'm on the 30th floor."

"I live in the penthouse."

The officer's face changed instantly. "What's your name, ma'am?"

"Diane Taylor." Diane replied slowly, fearful of what was to come. The officer reached for his walkie-talkie and nodded to Chandra.

"Please park the car and come with me." The officer strode away, speaking rapidly into the walkie-talkie. Chandra quickly parked, both women unsure of what to do.

After the preliminary, cursory introductions, Diane escorted two officers up to her penthouse, using her special key to access the floor. An uncomfortable silence settled in the elevator as the numbers ticked off the floors they were passing. 28...29...30...31...32.... The door opened with a ding and the four exited toward the penthouse door. Diane rushed to the entryway and tried the handle. It was locked.

"They didn't go through the door." The officer informed her, seeing the silent inquiry in her face. "They came up from the emergency stairs and cut in through the glass on your balcony." The officer pointed to the left toward the glass door that led to the balcony. A line of yellow police tape cordoned off the space from casual viewing. And, sure enough, there was a perfectly circular hole cut in the glass, evidenced by the slight breeze that fluttered a loose end of tape. The sight lent a rather eerie air to the situation and sent a chill down Diane's spine. She looked fearfully at the officer, her face tense.

"There's no one inside now, right? Someone checked?"

The officer smiled a little to allay her trepidation. "No, ma'am. It's all clear. Let's go take a look inside."

Diane got out her key and unlocked the door. The four walked in, eyes alert for anything out of place. Diane gasped when she saw her bedroom. All the drawers were open and her lovely clothes were spilled and crumpled in heaps on the floor. The room was in general disarray, but this fact wasn't what drained the color from Diane's face. The safe in her closet was standing open—and completely, hopelessly empty.

"My jewels! They're gone!" Diane raised a trembling hand to her mouth and sank onto her bed, her knees unable to support her weight any longer. The officer regarded her kindly, but still went about his job.

"Ma'am, I know it's late, but I need you to take an inventory of the things that are missing so we can report them. Does anyone live here with you?"

"No, just me."

"Do you have pictures of the contents of the safe?"

"The insurance company does." Diane stared at the safe, wringing her hands absent-mindedly.

The officer pulled out a pad and pencil and resumed his questions. "What time did you leave the apartment and where did you go?"

"I left—with Chandra—around 6 pm and we went to my boss house for his daughter's bridal shower. He owns this building"

"Did anyone know about your absence or is there anyone that you suspect who might have done this? Any friends or enemies who knows you have jewels?"

Diane rubbed her forehead. "No. I can't think of anyone." No one knows I have jewels in my place or in the safe except my penthouse owner.

"Well, it's too late to bring in detectives and a forensics team to collect evidence, but we're not able to let you spend the night here. Is it possible for you to stay with your friend tonight? That way you won't disturb any evidence. We can do the examination in the morning. We'll seal the apartment and post a guard. Does that sound all right?"

Diane glanced at Chandra, who nodded. "She can stay with me. We're about the same size so she can borrow clothes from me."

"Good. Then we'll let you know tomorrow when we need you here." The officer tipped an imaginary cap toward them.

On the way to Chandra's apartment, Chandra asked Diane, "Diane, do you want to call and tell Paul?"

"No, it's too late. I'll call him in the morning. It's his safe, you know. He kept his business papers in it. I hope he didn't leave anything important in it. I didn't even know the safe's combination."

Chandra looked at her in surprise. "But the jewels are yours?"

"Yes, I kept them in his safe instead of paying for a bank safe safety deposit box. Also I am lazy to go to the bank to take my jewelry when I need it for a party or occasions".

"You're lucky they are insured. Let's try to get some sleep. You can use the room Mom uses when she visits. She keeps it really tidy. If you need a drink or anything just go and get it in the fridge. You do you want any drink or anything"?

"No thanks. Thank you for letting me stay here tonight, Chandra."

Chapter 10

Dave and Diane Meet

The next morning, while Diane slept soundly, Detective Dave Merko, even more handsome in person than on TV, entered the apartment building. Taller than the average man, he was an intimidating figure as he strode purposefully toward the security guard station, his partner Sue Cooper trailing. Sue was an average-looking woman of 28, with a good head on her shoulders and a joy of teasing anyone she met. Dave flipped open his badge and flashed it before the eyes of a very nervous Trevor.

"I'm Detective Merko and this is Detective Cooper. We're here to investigate last night's burglary and we'd like to ask you a few questions. Were you on duty at the time?"

For as scared as Trevor appeared, he kept his composure credibly. "No, sir, it was Tom, who works the night shift. He'd have been on from 8 pm to 8am."

"Do you have any contact information for him?"

"The company log has his phone number and address."

Sue, seeing Dave start to wander away, checking out the lobby, quickly stepped in, armed with a notepad. "Please give me both of your full names, addresses and phone numbers." Trevor rattled them off as Dave made a slow circle of the lobby, his eyes roving constantly.

"Where are the building security cameras located?" Dave asked.

"Four outside at ground level covering all sides of the building and one on each floor monitoring the elevator area and lobby." He pointed helpful fingers in the directions he was indicating. "These monitors behind me alternate all the cameras every minute. We record 24 hours a day." Dave and Sue watched the monitors for a few minutes, taking detailed notes. Sue leaned over and whispered something in Dave's ear. He smiled wryly.

"So, Trevor, when you're watching the TV you're not able to see the monitors, is that right?"

Trevor glanced at the TV rather guiltily. "Technically speaking, no, but we keep an eye on them regularly every two minutes or so."

Sue smiled rather arrogantly and Dave shook his head despairingly. "Get last night's recordings ready for us and we'll pick them up on our way out later. Could you call Diane Taylor and ask her to meet us at her apartment?"

"Sir, you need a key for the elevator to enter the penthouse". Trevor was opening a drawer and picking up a key.

"I think she's staying in room 306. I'll give her a call and let her know. Here's the elevator key to access the penthouse floor." Trevor held up a small gold key, which Sue took with a nod of thanks. The detectives headed for the elevator as Trevor made the call.

"What do you think Miss Taylor will be like?" Sue asked Dave curiously as they rode.

Dave shrugged uncaringly. "Probably some rich old lady that has ropes of pearls and is really annoyed at losing them." They arrived, the ding of the door cutting off further conversation. The glass door to the balcony was roped off with police tape and Dave gave it only a cursory glance before moving toward the door. He showed the uniformed guard his badge as Sue inspected the door.

"Look at these marks on the door. Maybe they tried the door first."

"Or maybe they were made before." Dave replied, his expert eyes taking in every detail. The elevator door opened just then and the vision of Diane stepping out blew every preconception Dave had about he right out of the water. She had dressed quickly that morning and her hair was in a flyaway ponytail, but little dark wisps framing her rosy cheeks gave her a soft, morning look that quite charmed Dave. Her overall beauty and large, exquisite eyes had Dave frozen for a few seconds before he remembered where he was and what he was there to do.

"Miss Taylor?" He asked, approaching her, only to see that she was even more captivating up close.

"Yes." Diane replied, thinking that the television cameras had not done this man any justice. She hadn't been prepared for this specimen with rugged good looks and a tall, strong body.

"I'm Detective Dave Merko, and this is my partner, Sue Cooper." Dave and Sue both displayed their badges for Diane's inspection. There was a comradely sparkle in Dave and Diane's eyes as they watched each other.

"I saw you on the news a while ago, didn't I?"

"Most likely for our last robbery case."

"You solved that, didn't you?" Diane asked, already knowing the answer.

Dave grinned proudly. "Yes, ma'am. And we'll get whoever did this, too."

"Oh please, call me Diane. Both of you." Diane included Sue

in her dazzling smile, but the flirtatious look in her eyes was directed squarely at Dave. "Would you like me to open the door?"

Sue handed her a pair of gloves. "Yes, but please wear these. We want any fingerprints to go undisturbed." Sue was wise and observant, and the smiles and looks between Dave and Diane had not gone unnoticed. She smiled to herself, tucking that information away for later ammunition against Dave. The three then entered the living room and took seats on Diane's cushy couches.

Dave looked down at his notes. "I need to ask you some questions for the record. I understand from the officer's notes from last night that yesterday you left about 6 pm. Is that correct?"

"Yes."

"You live alone?"

"Yes."

Dave's cell phone rang, causing him to let out a grunt of annoyance. He took the call, walking away to give him a certain amount of privacy while he spoke in low tones to whoever was on the other end. While he was talking he was looking at Diane and Diane was also looking at him. He hung up and returned to his seat. "Miss Taylor—Diane, our fingerprint expert and photographer are downstairs. Would you give them permission to come up?"

"Sure, I'll call security and let them know." Diane reached for a handset and made the call. Dave watched her admiringly, noting her slender fingers and graceful movements.

"All right, let's keep going. So you live alone." A knock interrupted Dave again. Sue, catching a look from Dave, jumped up and let in the fingerprint expert and photographer. After being shown around, they both got to work. With a wry smile, Dave started again. "Who else has keys to your apartment?"

"Just me. Oh, and the owner."

"No roommate?" Dave looked around, and then decided to push the point a little further seemingly forgetting he already knew the answer to his question. "You live alone in this big place?" Sue stifled a chuckle, knowing what Dave was fishing for. Diane saw through the façade and answered accordingly.

"No roommate. I never married, I don't have any kids, and I don't have a boyfriend. Does that answer all your questions?"

Dave flushed a little, glancing down at his bare left hand, knowing that Diane was doing the same. "More than enough. Do you have a list of what was taken?"

"It was just my jewels from the safe. All my paintings are still here. I really don't have anything else that has outstanding value lying around."

"What else was in the safe?"

"The safe belongs to my boss. I rent the apartment from him. Originally he was going to live here, so he bought the safe to keep his business important documents. When I asked him to keep my jewels, he let me keep my jewels in it along with whatever he had in it."

"You had only jewels, not cash or anything else?"

"Just jewels."

"Who else beside you and your boss knows the combination to the safe?"

"Only my boss, Paul Rittman."

"You don't know the combination?"

"No, like I said, it's his safe."

"I understand that your jewels are insured?"

"Yes, they are."

"How much are they insured for?"

"It is insured under my boss, Paul Rittman. He only knows the insured value."

"Have you informed your insurance company?"

"I'm waiting for my boss to show up."

As soon as she said that, the door opened as if on cue, Paul Rittman walked in, his face set with concern. "Diane! Are you okay?" Diane nodded, her face suddenly pale and tense. Dave and Sue made the obligatory introductions and showed Paul the damage. Anger flashed across his face as he surveyed the empty safe.

"Any leads or clues?" He asked Dave tightly.

"Not yet, sir. We should be able to find something from the fingerprint information and the security tapes. It's too early to tell yet. Can you tell me what you had in the safe?"

Paul paused for a minute, thinking hard. "Yes, I had a few legal and real estate documents. My lawyer has copies of them. I am not concerned about them. It her jewels I am concerned about."

"You are the only person with the combination to this safe?"

"That's correct."

"Do you have the combination written down anywhere?"

"No, I have it memorized. I have a good memory and I don't write important numbers anywhere ".

"And Miss Taylor had her jewels in the safe as well...?"

"Yes. Only her jewels not mine and they're all insured."

"Anyone you think have access to your penthouse beside Miss. Taylor?

"Security guards have access to the penthouse floor but not inside the penthouse".

The fingerprint expert and the photographer returned just then, their arms laden with their equipment and their faces absent of the normally excited expression that marked singular success in their findings. "We're done here." The photographer spoke up.

"Anything interesting?"

The finger printer stepped forward. "I found some prints on the safe that weren't very clear. The window was clean, but I think I got some good ones from the door. I'll need to get the prints of anyone who has been in the apartment in the last six months to make some comparisons. I also found two foot- prints, a size ten and a size seven. The ten on the stairs all the way to the balcony and the seven only on the ground floor near the emergency door. The door has some kind of poly chemical spray on the alarm area. Looks like a clean job, by a professional." The man scratched his head, and then voiced what everyone had been thinking. "Looks like the Wynn Center robbery."

Dave looked at Paul and Diane. "He'll need your fingerprints, so unless there's any objection..." He let the sentence trail off, implying that they really didn't have a choice anyway.

Paul shrugged. "No problem here."

Diane nodded. "Sure." The fingerprinting was done quickly and efficiently, and the finger printer left right after. Paul and Diane held a quiet, unhurried conversation as they scrubbed the ink from their fingers. Sue watched them closely from across the room, noting the little looks and smiles they exchanged and the way Paul's hand trailed across Diane's waist as they stepped away from the sink.

Dave approached Paul again. "Sir, before you get the place cleaned up, you should ask the insurance company if they want to view the scene. Have them contact me for any reports they need. As soon as I find any new information I'll inform both of you." Dave handed a business card to each of them. With apparent regret on Dave's part as he cast one more intimate look at Diane, the two detectives left, their work done for the moment. They were quiet until the elevator door closed behind them and then Dave started on their customary initial debriefing.

"So, what do you think? Rittman? Or the Princess? Or both, or was it real?"

Sue smiled mischievously. "One thing I know for sure is that the Princess likes you. And I saw that dopey look on your face, too. Rittman's filthy rich—it's not likely that he'd take a risk with this kind of thing. But I do think that there's something going on between them. I wouldn't be surprised if he was having an affair with her."

Dave looked over at Sue, a serious look on his handsome features. "That safe wasn't broken into. It was opened by a person who knew the combination or by an expert. Diane doesn't know the combination."

"So where's she getting that kind of money for those jewels?" Sue challenged.

"That's the one that puzzling me. This is what I'm going to do: I'll check to see if the princess has any kind of records."

Sue grinned. "My, Dave, you certainly are a professional. I'm sure there's lots of personal information in those records." Dave looked unrepentant at being found out. "She's an attractive woman. And I've got a job to do and I'm going to do it right."

Sue opened the passenger door on the unmarked car. "Just attractive? Not sexy? And you do have a job to do. But, which one will you do first? Find the jewels or sleep with her?"

Dave opened the driver's door and winked. "Maybe both at the same time." Both shared a laugh as they pulled away.

Chapter 11

Questions

Diane sat on her couch, staring off into oblivion. Her thoughts whirled and spun in dizzying directions, not focusing on any particular thing as Paul paced, wearing a path in her soft carpet. He finally sat next to her.

"Who could have done this? I'll get to the bottom of this. At least the jewels were insured. You don't have to worry about that, Diane."

Diane smiled understandingly at Paul. "I'm not worried about the jewels. I'm worried about you."

"I only had a few dollars in that safe. Nothing enough to worry about."

"That's not what I'm worried about. I'm worried that your wife and kids will find out about our relationship."

Paul looked puzzled. "How?"

"You know the media. Those reporters will snoop and ask questions until they find some dirt on us."

Paul was quiet for a moment, pondering the wisdom of what Diane said. " Then I guess we should keep a low profile until this gets cleared up. Maybe I shouldn't aggravate the police."

Diane stroked his back. "You know it's going to be hard. But we have to do it."

Paul sighed and stood, smoothing out the creases in his slacks. "Let me go to the office and take care of the insurance and arrange to get the window fixed. You stay here and relax. Don't go anywhere today." He kissed her on the forehead rather absentmindedly and left. Diane curled up on the couch and flipped on the TV. The news was on, and the familiar face of the on-scene female reporter filled the screen.

"The burglary in the hi-rise apartment complex was the first for a building owned by the successful developer Paul Rittman. The theft was remarkably similar in execution to the burglary three months ago at the Wynn Center." The camera panned to Dave, who was back again in front of the cameras looking more at ease now in front of his own police station than a high-end skyscraper. Veronica eagerly posed the first questions to him.

"Detective Merko, are you confident that you will solve this mystery? Do you have any clues?"

"I am confident that, like the other case, this one will be solved."

Diane smiled. "Okay smart detective go and get my jewels".

Dave sat at his desk, scanning through documents on his computer. Sue walked in unannounced and perched on the edge of his desk. "So, anything interesting?"

"Rittman's rich with a capital R. He owns buildings in Seattle and Hawaii. Princess has done pretty well for herself too. She has $12,000 money in her bank account but not enough to check how she got it. She is a well known architect. But there's no record of anything even remotely suspicious about either. Did you check on the security guys?"

"I checked the security guys and they don't even have a single traffic violation. No motive, no agenda. They're clean."

Dave typed in a command, sighing. "Let's wait for the fingerprints and the analysis from the recordings of the security camera to focus our investigation." Just then, Chief of Police Ron Matthews strode into Dave's office, a stern look on his face. Chief Ron Matthews was a big man, 58 years old and looking forward to his retirement when he turned 60. He had been with the Seattle police department for 30 years, which was plenty of time for everyone under him to respect his judgment and leadership. And even the greenest rookie learned quickly to steer clear when he stroked that long gray mustache.

"What do you have on the robbery?"

"Nothing yet, Chief." Dave answered respectfully. "I'm waiting for the results of the fingerprints and reports from the security tape. I'm also checking other leads."

Ron stroked his mustache dangerously.

"Well, don't just sit there! Go to the lab and see how they're doing. I'm getting pressure from the newspapers, the mayor, and Senator Thomas. This is not like the coins case. Powerful people involved in this case. They want to sole this case ASAP. Mayor, a powerful senator and rich and connected Paul Rittman want know who did it?. But, I want to know before any new reporters or other. You get it ? It's not even lunchtime , I am getting phone calls every minute. If you don't have any good news for me by 9 am tomorrow, I'm putting someone else in charge."

Dave stood quickly, an irritated look flashing across his face. "I understand. I'll give you a report tomorrow at 9:00 am sharp." Matthews nodded curtly and left just as abruptly as he had come. Sue whistled quietly, feeling bad about her nonchalant attitude.

Dave looking at Sue with angry face, "You check the lab and I'll go snoop around to see if your Diane and Rittman have anything going on."

Sue feel bad and said "Okay Dave, don't take it out on me".

"I am sorry, you understand the pressure I am in. Thanks."

Dave flashed a grateful look and headed for the finger print lab. There an analyst was working on a computer. He looked up and saw Dave coming.

"Oh, Dave, good timing!"

"What've you got for me?"

"I assume you want details. I checked the fingerprints on the safe. Only Rittman's. Whoever opened the safe must have used gloves. Other fingerprints in the apartment belong to Taylor and Rittman. The size ten footprints are the same from the ground floor to the balcony and inside the penthouse. The size seven stopped at the ground floor. Looks like size seven belonged to the lookout guy—same as the coin robbery case." The analyst reached for an evidence collection bag and held it up for Dave's inspection. "We found traces of grass and bark on the footprints which match grass and bark from the surrounding area. I checked the poly chemical spray on the alarm system by the west emergency door. It didn't do anything. Maybe it was a diversion."

For the first time that day, Dave looked puzzled. "That's interesting. Thank you, e-mail me the report. Who checked the security camera recording?"

The analyst pointed to a back corner. "Claire Rivers."

Dave walked into a small office where Claire, a woman about 30 with remarkably curly hair, was working on a video system. "Hi Claire, did you have a chance to check the Rittman's robbery recording?"

"Yes, I did. I was just about to send you an email. The recording is dark and fuzzy, so it's not clear enough to positively identify anything. A shadowy figure enters the west door at 10:30 pm and exits at 11:14 pm. that's all I can see. My question is, why didn't the alarm go off at 10: 30?"

Dave shrugged. "Good question. Were you able to get any visual on the person?"

"I used all the techniques I know. It's just too dark and fuzzy. I can let you see the tape if you want."

Dave shook his head. "Did you say there was only one person?"

"Yes, that's one thing that I know for sure. Same size person entering and exiting."

"Thanks. Keep working and let me know if you find anything, even something that seems insignificant."

Claire gave him a small salute and smiled. "Yes, sir!"

Chapter 12

Building Security Guards Investigation

At about 9 pm that same night, Dave visited the security guard on duty in the building's security office." You were the one here at the time of the robbery?"

"Yes, sir." The guard seemed calmer than he had been during the previous interview. He was now in his element as the questions centered on his line of work. "I have a few questions for you, but first I want to see your security alarm control room."

"The alarm control center is in the back next to the ladies room. We don't have the key—only the alarm company has it. Most of the system can be accessed from this desk—if you know how. We aren't licensed technicians, but it's mostly automated anyway. And we never leave our posts, so no one can mess with it."

Dave jotted down a few notes as he glanced around at the station. "Has anyone gone to the control room recently, to the best of your knowledge?" Tom shook his head. "No, sir."

"Do you have the alarm company's number?"

"Yes, sir." Tom produced a business card with the company address and phone number on it from a pile of papers and handed it to Dave.

"How long have you been working here?"

A look of pride crossed Tom's face. "I've been here since the day it opened eight, years ago."

"How long have you known Diane Taylor?"

Tom thought of the stunning outfits Diane had worn in the past and smiled toothily. "She moved here about five years ago. She's an architect for Mr. Rittman."

Dave hesitated, and then plunged into the territory he was reluctant to explore. "Tell me about the relationship between Paul Rittman and Diane Taylor." He was unexplainably relieved at the surprised look that appeared unfeigned on Tom's features.

"Well, I don't know, sir. They go for lunch and dinner together a lot. They're always talking business when I see them." He recalled a sudden memory. "I met his family when I delivered something to their house once. They're really nice people. Miss Taylor's nice, too." He added, making sure Dave knew that there were no hard feelings between him and anyone involved.

"When was the first time you saw the intruder?"

"About 11:15 pm. As soon as I heard the alarm I looked at the monitors and I saw a person in dark clothes coming out of the west emergency door."

"According to our tapes, we saw the same person entering at 10:30 pm. Why did that escape your notice?"

A defensive note crept into Tom's voice. "Sir, the alarm didn't go off at that time. To keep our eyes on all the monitors at all times simply isn't possible. My eyes sometimes hurt because I stare at the monitors so much."

"Were you watching TV at the time?"

"We leave it on all the time so we don't fall asleep. I was probably watching it." Tom admitted.

"And you saw only one person? Not two?" Dave pressed.

"Just one."

"Have there been any other thefts here, ever?"

"Not to my knowledge, sir, in eight years. This place is ritzy and the rent is really high. We keep a close eye on things like pizza deliveries and visitors."

"Who has keys to the outside doors?"

"Just us two guards and the office manager."

"I met Trevor this morning. How would you characterize him?"

Tom grinned. "He's my brother-in-law. He's a good guy."

"Okay, that's all I need now. Here's my number. Call me if you remember anything else."

"Yes, sir." Tom pocketed the business card and watched in relief as Dave left.

Chapter 13

The Rittman's

The food was delicious as always, when cooked by their Italian chef, but Lisa Rittman's thoughts were far away from anything she was putting in her mouth. Lisa was eating dinner with her husband, who was seated at the opposite end of the table, daughter Christina, son Jason, two of their friends and Christina's future husband. But she felt as if she was eating alone. Lisa was looking straight at Paul while eating and thinking about Diane, the robbery, Christina's shower, how beautiful Diane looked and the closeness of Paul and Diane. How did she have all those jewels? She is just an architect. Is Paul having an affair? He is buying all these jewels for her?

Her mind faded away to the past. After 25 years of marriage, they had grown apart, and Lisa hated it. It had been different when they first met. Paul was young, just 25, and at the beginning of his career. Lisa was two years older than him. Paul worked as a construction supervisor for her father, Martin, and became like a son to him. He was around all the time, having dinner with Lisa and Martin's family, looking after Martin's construction business when Martin was sick or out of town and eventually, falling in love with Lisa. Martin couldn't be happier when Paul asked Lisa out for the first time. Lisa, after a brief hesitation, let herself fall in love with a man that she saw as responsible, hard working, warm, caring, and fun loving. It wasn't until after their marriage a year after their first date that Lisa became acquainted with the side of Paul that was ruthless, harsh, and power-hungry. Two years almost to the day after Paul and Lisa were married, Martin died in a construction accident, leaving the building business to his family and Paul, who quickly clawed his way to the top. Their marriage had dwindled from that point. They had two children together, Christina and Jason, but after that, the exciting, romantic life that Lisa had eagerly anticipated had evaporated. She was determined to make the best of it, though. She believed that if she kept living her life as one would say normal and showed her unfailing love to Paul, he would some day love her again.

The dinner was over and the children and friends were gone. Paul was sitting in their library, sipping his favorite brandy and reading the sports page. Lisa walked into the library and sat opposite to him

Lisa looked straight at Paul. "How did Diane get all those expensive jewels?"

"She told me that she inherited them from her grandmother. Her grandfather was a gem merchant or something." Paul kept his eyes on his paper, replying quietly.

"Why did she keep them in your office safe?"

Paul shrugged, glancing at Lisa and quickly looking away again. "She asked me and I couldn't refuse. They were important to her."

"Is she doing okay?"

"I think so."

"I'm going to call and make sure." Lisa got up and went to the phone in the library and dialed Diane's number.

"Hello?"

Lisa tucked the phone between her shoulder and ear. "Hi, Diane, this is Lisa Rittman. I heard the bad news and just wanted to see if you were okay."

"I'm fine, thanks so much for asking."

"My husband told me that your jewels are insured under our policy, so don't worry about it,"

"Yes, Paul—Mr. Rittman told me."

"The press is thinking that they were my jewels and they're knocking on our door all the time. We're keeping the gate locked now. Are you safe there alone? You're welcome to stay with us for a few days."

Diane's voice sounded grateful, but rather nervous on the other end. "Oh no, I'm fine. I stayed with Chandra last night and there's a guard here for a couple weeks. Thank you anyway."

"No problem. Call anytime if you need anything."

"Thanks, I will."

Lisa hung up and headed back to Paul. Paul was just clearing his last mouthful of brandy as she sat back down at her seat.

"Done already?" She asked with a smile. Paul nodded and left the library. Lisa sighed to herself. She had come to expect nothing more than the very least necessary to communicate. They never talked anymore, just about the kids' school and activities and sometimes work. Paul was kind to her—he had never been anything but—but the fire had died long ago. Paul fulfilled his husbandly duties rather coolly, but Lisa knew he was getting his gratification other places. She was no dummy—she saw the looks between Paul and Diane and knew how much time they spent together. There was many a night when Paul didn't come home from the office and several weekends to Hawaii which Diane, as his chief architect, had of course needed to accompany him. Lisa, no matter how hard she tried, simply couldn't fall out of love with him, even though she knew that the man she had originally fallen for didn't exist to her anymore.

Christina adored her father with the passion only a true daddy's girl could own. In her eyes, he could do no wrong. He was her example in every situation, and had coached her into her now-successful life. She had turned out rather like him too, in temperament and business practices. She did anything she could to get ahead, destroying friendships and other's dreams as she went. She was personable, outgoing, and happy—traits that endeared her to people that were not whom she considered beneath her. She saw her marriage to the senator's son as a crowning success in her life, but Lisa could never forget what her daughter had done to poor Julie Stewart to get him. He had been engaged to Julie, but Christina had flirted and manipulated her way into his blind heart and left Julie by the wayside. During all the wedding plans, Lisa had just had to grit her teeth and bear it with a smile that she didn't feel, knowing she had lost a good friend in Rita Stewart because of her daughter's actions.

Jason was Christina's polar opposite. He was kind, gentle, and had a wonderful sense of humor that warmed Lisa's heart. He was tenderhearted and hated how his father and sister treated others. He had always been determined to treat people how they deserved to be treated, although he had enough of his father in him to treat people rather unkindly if he thought they deserved it. He loved his mother fiercely, and protected her from his father's coolness as only a 17-year-old boy can do. He had a large, diverse group of friends, and a loyal, little dog that adored him. He always brought great joy and encouragement to his mother.

Lisa sighed again as she sat in the library and looking at the photos of her marriage and the children. The house seemed so quiet and empty. Paul was upstairs in his office working on who-knows-what, Christina was with her fiancé, and Jason was over at a friend's house. Only Minnie, Jason's little dog, was there to make the house a little cozier. Lisa laughed bitterly at the thought of just a dog keeping her company. She caught her thoughts before they spiraled downward into a depressive mood and straightened her shoulders purposefully. She would pick herself up and try again, like she had been doing for 25 years. She would make it work, no matter what.

Chapter 14

Dave on the Hunt

The bar was dark, full of cigarette smoke, and packed with rough-looking people who kept their eyes slanted downward and their glasses tilted up as Dave walked in. The bartender, who was cleaning the counter with a damp rag, watched warily as Dave slid onto a stool. His heavy eyelids and large paunch belied the fact that he was one of the most informed people in the criminal circle in Seattle. He had been involved in multiple crimes, but no one had ever been able to pin anything on him. He was rich as a king, but kept his bartender job as a way to stay in the "business."

"What brings you here, detective?" Jed asked suspiciously. Dave had been here before, but never with good news. "What did I do this time?"

"Just give me a beer. Not the illegal stuff, Coors is fine."

Jed made a face and filled a cold glass with the light foamy liquid. "That's funny. So you just came to hang out and have a drink?"

Dave shrugged vaguely. "Yes and no. I need some information about jewels."

Jed resumed his wiping with vigor. "I don't deal with jewels."

Dave's voice stayed calm and quiet, but took on an edge.

"Yeah, but you know someone who does. Someone has been spending heavily quite and lately been talking about a big deal. I know you've got information."

Jed rested his beefy hands on the counter and looked Dave straight in the eye. "Why should I level with you? I don't know what you're up to, what kind of knowledge you want."

"I'm investigating a burglary. Several thousands of dollars in jewelry was stolen and I think one of your junkie 'customers' had something to do with it."

Jed grinned, displaying silver-capped teeth. "So, what you're saying is that all my customers are thieves and trash. I guess that makes you one too." He gestured toward Dave's half-empty mug.

Dave's fist tightened around the frosty glass, dripping condensation down the sides onto the counter. "I'm just telling you to keep your eyes and ears open for any information that you can give me. And you will deliver."

Jed snorted disdainfully. "What's in it for me? Why should I do your dirty work?"

Dave looked pointedly at a row of unlabeled bottles half-hidden on a dusty rack. "Let me put it this way. I can get a search warrant to check your joint for illegal drugs and booze. You prefer that?"

Jed considered the options before him. "Well, since you put it that way..." His voice became sarcastic. "It would be my pleasure."

"Thank you for your cooperation." Dave replied dryly. Jed just mumbled something and waved a hand toward the door.

A tall and slimy looking man - insurance agent named Mike Sinessi—with thick eyeglasses, a simple casual suit and a leather bag in his hand walked inside the Seattle police headquarters early the next morning. The young police officer at the front desk greeted him with a friendly smile.

"I'm here to see Detective Dave Merko." Mike told him and handed the officer his business card.

The officer stuck to what he had been told to say. "Is there anything I can do to help?"

"This is about the jewelry theft. I really need to speak to Mr. Merko only."

The officer again did what he was told. "I'll call him for you. You need to sign in this book for our records." He slid a ledger with lines of many different names toward Mike and disappeared around the corner. Mike signed his name with a flourish that he had always been proud of and when he had put the pen back, Dave was standing in front of him, a curious light in his eye.

"I'm Detective Merko, what can I do for you?"

Mike stuck out his hand. "I'm Mike Sinessi with the Sun Insurance Company. I was told to check in with you about the penthouse robbery."

"Good. Come with me. Let's go to my office." Mike followed Dave back to his office where they both took a seat. Dave started the conversation. "How much are the jewels worth?"

Mike hesitated. "Roughly fife million. These are investment quality gems. The replacement value now could be up to eight million." "Whose name is on the policy?"

"It's in Miss Diane Taylor name. But all items were insured and paid for by Mr. Rittman—because it's his safe and his building. The insurance costs were lower because of Mr. Rittman's financial position. Therefore, it was wise for her to insure it under Rittman."

"Everything was insured at the same time?"

"No. Every year, another piece was added, for the last six

years."

"I wonder where she's getting the money to buy that kind of jewelry every year." Dave mused out loud. "She's just an architect."

"That information is not available to the insurance company, or I would tell you." Mike said with a shrug.

"Any other claims on this robbery?"

"$6,000 in cash was also claimed."

Dave pursed his lips and frowned. "That's interesting. That hadn't been mentioned before. Whose money is that?"

"Mr. Rittman's, I believe. His business's petty cash policy allows him to keep up to $10,000 in the safe."

"Have you spoken to either of them?"

"Yes, Mr. Rittman called us the next day and I talked to both him and Miss Taylor. I also inspected the penthouse."

Dave leaned back in his chair, satisfied for the most part. "So, Mr. Sinessi, what information do you want from us?"

"I'll need a updated status update on the case and a look at the investigation file."

Dave complied, handing Mike a file folder that was, in Dave's estimation, regrettably thin. Mike flipped through the contents, closely examining interviews and photographs. "There isn't much to see, but this will give you enough information about what happened that night. I'll need photographs and the exact values of all the jewels from you."

"I'll send you a copy of all that later today." Mike replied, still poring over the file contents. "So, according to your report, there were footprints and a person running from the building. The alarm only went off at 11:14 pm and not 10:32 pm. Mr. Rittman and Miss Taylor were both at a party with a lot of people around them at the time of the robbery. Only Mr. Rittman knows the combination to the safe. The safe wasn't broken, so someone got the right numbers or it was done by professionals."

Dave nodded. "That's about right."

Mike thought of something. "Did you check why the alarm system didn't go off at 10:32 pm?"

"Yes, I checked with the security alarm company. According to them, they checked the control panel and there was no tampering of any kind. It's a mystery so far,"

Mike stood and handed Dave a card. "This is my business card. Please call me anytime when you get any news."

"I certainly will." Dave replied.

Chapter 15

The Puzzle

Diane flipped on the television in her penthouse. The robbery had made the news, and she was eager to watch the broadcast. The anchorman was talking as she switched to the local news channel.

"According to the insurance company, thousands of dollars worth of jewels that belonged to the Rittman family were stolen. Detective Dave Merko is leading the investigation and our Melissa Hill talked to him this morning." The scene changed to Melissa and Dave sitting in two chairs facing each other.

"Do you have any idea who might have done this?" Melissa asked Dave, her face a practiced study of concern.

""We have footprints and footage from the security camera. It's too early to say anything more."

"This job sounds like the robbery which you solved only a few weeks ago. Were they done by the same people? Are you confident that you will catch the culprit?"

Dave smiled a little. "That is my job and I am good at what I do."

"You seem very confident." Melissa clearly expected an explanation.

"Well, we have some strong leads and solid evidence. I see no reason to be otherwise."

Diane sat in her living room poured herself a drink with a smile. The news ended there and moved on to the next story. Diane shut off the TV and went to bed.

Chief of police Ron Matthews was sitting at his desk talking on the phone when Dave and Sue knocked. He waved them in as he finished his call. "So what do you have for me?"

Dave leaned back in his chair and cleared his throat. "Let me explain this in detail so that you understand completely where we stand on this case."

"Shoot." Ron tapped his fingers 0n his desk and regarded Dave steadily.

"We have security tapes that show one person entering the west door at 10:32 pm and leaving through the same door at 11:14 pm. The alarm wasn't tripped when the person entered, only when they left at 11:14 pm. That's just the first puzzle." Ron nodded, intrigued. Dave continued. "I checked with the alarm company and there's no sign of tampering. We have two sets of footprints, a size seven and a size ten. The size ten leads from the west emergency door up to the penthouse balcony and inside the penthouse. The size seven stopped right at the west floor. There's two different shoe prints but only one shadow on the security tapes. That's the second puzzle." Dave looked at Sue, who took the silent cue.

"The safe was opened with no signs of force used. $5 million worth of jewels belonging to Diane Taylor was taken and $6,000 in cash belonging to Paul Rittman was also missing. The only fingerprints on scene belong to Rittman and Taylor."

Dave looked back . "I checked on Diane Taylor. She and Rittman often go to Hawaii on business. Rittman owns a suite hotel there where they both collaborated on the building and its completion. My biggest question for her right now is: How did she get that much money for jewelry?"

Ron thought for a minute. "This case sounds similar to the Wynn Center, but both of those boys are in prison right now, waiting for trial. Someone's doing a copycat job here. What's your plan, Dave?"

"One—I'm going to meet with Diane Taylor to find out how she got all those jewels. Two—circulate the pictures of the jewels to all police and FBI sites to see if any of them have been recently sold and to have them watch for future sales. Three—check on the footprints and suspects. Four—check the neighborhood for anyone who might have seen anything unusual at the time of the theft and see if any parking or traffic tickets were issued during that time in and around the surrounding area."

"Good plan. Now, move on it—fast. Rittman is a powerful man and he's got just as powerful friends. I have a lunch meeting with the mayor and I'm sure that Rittman will be there. We have to be extra careful to not release anything to the press. Understand?"

Dave and Sue acquiesced silently with nods. Ron waved them back out the door and they obeyed, pulling the door shut behind them. They were half way down the hall again when Dave spoke up.

"I'm going to go talk to the princess."

Sue glanced at him knowingly. "You really like her, don't you? She's sexy, lives in a luxury penthouse, set up to collect big-time on the insurance, and very successful. What else do you need?"

Dave looked at her with a dangerous gleam in his eye. "What do you know about my needs? I'm focused on solving this case, not on what I need."

Sue held up her hands in mock surrender. "Okay, I'm just kidding. You're serious, aren't you?"

"Serious about what?"

"You tell me. The case or the girl?"

Dave shrugged his thoughts far away with a beautiful woman that had preoccupied his mind for many hours. "Of course, the case. You don't respect my tactics, do you?"

"Okay, I believe you for now. Let's wait and see." Sue walked away with a smile.

Chapter 16

The First Love Connection

The next morning, Dave walked into the Rittman building and approached the receptionist at the desk. The receptionist smiled broadly—it wasn't every day that a gorgeous man stood before her.

"Can I help you?" She purred sweetly, forgetting for the moment she was married and almost a grandmother.

"I'm Detective Dave Merko, and I'm here to see Diane Taylor." Dave replied, all business and trying not to notice the suggestion in the receptionist's heavily made-up eyes. The receptionist shrugged as if it were her loss and reached for the phone. After a quick conversation, she turned back to Dave, who was staring at his shiny shoes.

"She'll be down in just a moment, sir."

"Thanks." Dave puttered around for fifteen minutes or so, and then Diane was in front of him, exuding life and warmth through every pore. She looked remarkable, in an attractive green skirt with matching jacket and shimmering gold eye shadow. She extended a slim hand towards his in greeting. "You have good news for me, detective?"

"Miss Taylor, I'm sorry to have to bother you right now, but I need to ask you some more questions."

Diane glanced at him flirtatiously. "But, detective, you haven't answered my question yet."

Dave smiled. "Ma'am, I'm sorry to say that we don't have any new information for you. We're still checking the finger prints and shoe prints."

"Oh, please call me Diane. I was actually taking a lunch break. Would you like to join me? You can ask those questions while we're eating."

"Sounds good to me Diane." Dave and Diane shared a smile. "Will Mr. Rittman be joining us?"

"No, he's out to lunch with the mayor." Diane's face dropped slightly. "Why, do you need to ask him questions too? I was hoping to have you all to myself." A winning smile flashed across her face as she slid her arm through his. Dave just laughed and patted her hand as it lay on his arm. Diane led the way just a block down the street to a small Italian restaurant where a waiter immediately showed them to a private table for two, sweeping a 'Reserved' sign off the tablecloth as they were seated.

Dave looked across the table at Diane in disbelief. "How did you reserve a table that fast?"

Diane smiled. "This table is always reserved for Mr. Rittman and me." She folded her arms on the table and leaned slightly toward him; affording him a perfect—and distracting—view of her cleavage. "So, what do you want to know?"

"I met with the insurance company investigator yesterday and I need to clarify a few things. When this much money is involved, we question everyone. According to the insurance company, the value of the jewels is more than $5 million. That day you said I don't know. May I ask why you didn't know the value of the insured jewels?"

Diane toyed with her water glass. "They were all gifts and Mr. Rittman—he got them appraised—insured them himself. I didn't know the exact amount, so I couldn't tell you."

Dave looked surprised. " All gifts? From whom?"

Diane looked down, feeling strangely embarrassed. "I don't have to answer that question, but I can only tell you that gifts are mostly from Paul Rittman—my boss --as a reward for my best architectural designs...a bonus of sorts."

"No one mentioned the money in the safe. Why is that?"

Diane looked puzzled for the first time. "I didn't have any money in the safe. You'll have to ask Paul about that." A silence, surprisingly comfortable, fell between them as they ate their pasta. Diane broke it first.

"So, tell me, Mr. Merko, how long have you been a detective?"

"Call me Dave, please. I've been on the police force for six years. I started as an assistant detective and two years ago became a full detective."

"Hey, we have something in common!"

"What's that?"

"Six years ago I graduated and started to work as an architect."

"Why an architect?"

"Architecture is an art and a science. I love to create. When you are designing a building you are creating something. Also you have to know the technical knowledge of designing a building. Architecture is my passion and life. And I'm good at it too. You have to have passion to succeed in anything you do.

When you design a building and it actually gets built, it becomes yours. Every time you pass that building, you feel like a proud mother, or a sort of god. Have you seen the new library in Belleview?"

"Yes, did you design that? Diane nodded her head. Diane laughed a little, feeling uncomfortable. "Don't ask me about architecture I will keep on talking".

Dave continued. "Okay, let's change the subject. Where are you originally from? I mean, you have a little touch of a Southern accent."

"Oh, I do? You're right. I was born in Mississippi in a small town. My father worked in a paper company as a pipe fitter and my mom was a nurse. My father worked the night shifts and my mother worked days. Mom got fed up with my father working at night. Some times he worked seven days a week, I mean seven nights straight. Then, at the hospital where mother worked, she fell in love with a patient. I was only eight at that time. So mother left my father and took me with her to New York. So my stepfather brought me up mostly in New York with mom. He gave me lots of support and advice. He encouraged me to study and find a profession to get interested in and to learn to study with passion and said that is how I would find success. I like to create, so I became interested in architecture and I really enjoy it."

"So how did you end up in Seattle?"

"Oh, I was looking for a job and a real estate corporation, Weyerhaeuser Company here in Seattle hired me. I like Seattle's mountains and the ocean and the cool climate". So I decided to stay in the Seattle area.

"How did you end up with Mr. Rittman?"

"Is this part of your investigation?"

"No, no, just my curiosity."

"Have you heard that old cliché, curiosity killed the cat? Never mind. While I was working for Weyerhaeuser Company, I went to an architectural convention. It so happened Mr. Rittman was at the convention too. I gave a presentation of my architectural achievements and after my presentation Mr. Rittman approached me and told me how impressed he was with my work and how he admired my architectural talents. He said, any time you want to work as a chief Architect for me , just let me know and handed over his business card to me. After that, I did some investigation about Rittman Development Company; I liked the projects they were involved in and well, here I am. So, your turn. Why a detective?"

Dave arched an eyebrow teasingly. "I thought I came here to ask you questions. " Diane started to laugh. "Okay…I graduated with a degree in criminology. I was always fascinated with crime investigation. I enjoy solving the puzzles in crime and getting to put the criminals behind bars. I'm also good at what I do which means I will succeed in your case and put the person away."

"Is that a promise?"

"It's my duty and pleasure." Their eyes met, and held. Diane looked away first, her cheeks turning a soft pink.

"So tell me, what kind of pleasure do you get from it all? Is it just showing off and pretending to play macho or is it about being smart and putting the criminals away?"

Dave gave a puzzled smile and said, "Both. Is there something wrong with it?

"No, just wanted to know".

"Where are you from? Were you born in Seattle?"

"No I was born in Fresno, California. My mom is Scottish and my dad is mixed Hispanic and German. My dad was with the Fresno police force and I grew up watching him; he was strong, fearless. It empowered me to want to be just like him to work at putting criminals out of circulation. My mother didn't like the idea of me becoming a police officer. So to satisfy both, I became a detective. I completed my high school years at Clovis West High

School, which is still the best in Fresno, and graduated from California State University Fresno. We have something in common. I like Seattle too. The mountains, ocean and the cool weather. In Fresno, California the summer temperatures climb up to 120 degrees Fahrenheit. I hated the hot weather".

"I have a meeting in five minutes." Diane said regretfully. "You take your time finishing your meal and don't bother about the bill. It will go on the company account." Dave rose respectfully as Diane stood up.

"Are you trying to bribe me?" He asked seriously, but Diane heard the smile in his voice.

"Will it work?" She asked straight-faced. Dave just laughed and watched her go, his heart feeling lighter than it had in a long, long time.

Chapter 17

Powerful Meeting

The restaurant at the top of the Space Needle was luxurious, comfortable, and had a one-of-a-kind view of downtown Seattle. Only the wealthy and the privileged spent much time there among the spotless linens and sparkling crystal. So it was no surprise that Paul Rittman frequently darkened the doorway. He was there for lunch that day with Senator Thomas, Mayor Strickford, and Seattle police chief Ron Matthews. They all had plates heaping with aromatic, attractive food in front of them and a fantastic view out of the window spanning across the skyline of the downtown skyscrapers.

"So, Ron, how's the investigation going?" Mayor Strickford asked casually. Ron glanced at Paul before answering.

"I put my best detective, Dave Merko, on this case. I reviewed the progress right before I came here. We're doing our best to find the answer, sir." Ron was nervous. He didn't do these sorts of things very often—he was more at home chasing leads, pressuring the bad guys, and mostly staying in the background. Talking to the confident, charismatic mayor over an elegant, lunch in a ritzy restaurant certainly wasn't in his comfort zone.

The mayor leaned back in his chair, tapping his fingertips together. If Ron was uncomfortable, then Strickford was completely at ease. He had gotten to his position of power by charming some people and putting others in the hot seat. He was equally loved and hated by those who knew him, and mostly loved by those who didn't. He wasn't really a kind man; rather, he was a man that was callous and only concerned with making it to the top. He had Ron in his vice-like a grip—he wanted results, and results he would get, even if it meant Ron would lose the position he had worked so hard to get.

"Ron, I would really like this case to be solved much quicker than the other one was. Three months? We don't want the press hounding Mr. Rittman and his family." The mayor looked expectantly at Ron, who was tempted to run a finger around the collar that suddenly seemed much tighter than it had been. Paul nodded gratefully, choosing to ignore Ron's discomfort. Ron looked strained. "I personally will be on top of this case and will inform you as soon as we know who the culprit. is" The mayor then focused on his food, seeming to accept that answer—for the time being. Now it was Paul's turn to be grilled, but by the senator and not the mayor. Ron actually felt grateful for the fact that it was only the mayor putting the pressure on him. Paul was suddenly more ill at ease than he had been the whole time.

"Paul, how long has this girl architect Diane been working for you?"

"About six years." Paul prayed they wouldn't see past the forced casualness of his answers and see the truth of the affair. "She's a great architect."

The senator smiled, but Paul only saw a shark in those gleaming teeth. "She may be a great architect, but it is possible that she may be hanging around with the wrong people. I saw her at your place that day, Christina's shower day and I didn't like her dress or the way she was looking and talking to you. Keep an eye on her. You are going to be my son's father-in-law, and with the elections coming up, one small character flaw in any family members will be enough to bring me down. Just be careful."

Paul looked serious. "I understand, Senator. I'll keep a close eye on her and if I hear she's been keeping bad company I'll terminate her employment immediately. You can be sure of that."

Chapter 18

A Lead

In Dave's office, the phone rang shrilly. Dave picked up the receiver.

"This is detective Merko."

"Detective, this is Jed from the bar."

Dave grabbed for a scrap of paper and a pen. "What do you have?"

Jed's voice was low and husky, and hard to hear over a loud clamor of voices and pulsing music in the background. "I overheard an interesting conversation last night. A guy was bragging about an easy money job he did a couple days ago. I don't know if this has anything to do with your robbery case."

"Tell me more about the job." Dave pushed. "Did he have a lot of money to spend?"

"According to him, he just sat in a building for a few minutes and he was paid good money for it. He had more than enough to buy rounds of beer for four to five people all night long."

"Do you know his name or address?"

Jed chuckled, but there was no mirth in his laugh. "Man, I don't go tuck him in at night. I don't know where he lives. But I heard he hangs around a lot at the Paolo Bar on forth Street. Ask the bartender there for Con-Man Peter."

"If his nick name is Con-Man Peter, how do you know he's not just telling you another one of his stories this time?"

"I'm not the detective, you are. You can check him out or leave it. It's your call. You ask me for some information and I gave it to you."

"Okay, cool down, I will check him out."

Dave walked into the Paolo Bar, senses on the alert. The bar— it was actually more of a strip joint—was full of smoke, flashing lights, and girls on poles. The bartender gave Dave a suspicious look as Dave leaned on the counter. He was too clean-cut to be a customer here, and he didn't seem distracted even the tiniest bit by the gyrating, erotic movements of the girls around him. His reservations were confirmed when Dave swiftly flashed him a look at his police badge.

"What do you want?" The bartender growled.

"I'm looking for Con-Man Peter." Dave saw the shutters dropping over the bartender's eyes. "Jed sent me." A reluctant look came over the big man's face. He pointed toward a dark corner.

"That's him in the blue shirt."

"Thanks." Dave strode toward the bald, mean-looking man in the corner who was easily 80 pounds overweight and was studying a blonde dancer with a cruel look in his eyes. Dave dropped into the seat next to him. "Hey, Peter."

Peter turned slowly to look at Dave, a beer bottle dangling from his fat fingers. "Do I know you?"

Dave showed his badge, watching as Peter's expression changed from apprehension to fear and then to anger. "I need to talk to you." He motioned toward a back door. "Outside."

Peter rose slowly, the chair creaking from his girth. He tucked a bill into the blonde's waistband and led the way to the door. Dave glanced away—Peter bolted out the door. Dave sighed and took chase. He caught him easily and shoved the big man up against a wall. Peter was already sweating profusely from the run.

"What do you want?" He asked in a voice that held an unmistakable edge of fright. "I'll get your badge for police brutality. I know my rights."

Dave pressed him harder into the wall. "Stop shouting and tell me why you ran."

Peter's eyes glittered belligerently. "I don't like pigs, that's why."

Dave arched an eyebrow dangerously. "You want to go to the station or you going to answer my questions?"

"What do you want to know from me?"

"Tell me about the easy money you made a few days ago." Dave let Peter go, but kept a hand on his holster to let him know he meant business.

"What easy money, what job?"

"Okay, let's go to the station. Maybe that'll help you remember."

Peter held up his hands in surrender. "Okay, okay. I was told to go into a building and wait for a few minutes and then come out. I was paid 200 bucks for that. I didn't do anything else."

"Who gave you the job?"

"This Mexican guy, Caficio. Two days ago, he saw me having a drink at the bar and he came and sat next to me and asked me if I could do a small job at 10:30 PM that night. He paid me right there, so I took it."

"Where did you do this job?"

"He drove me to a building and told me to wear black overalls and a ski mask to hide my face. Then he gave me a key and told me to open the door and wait inside for 45 minutes. He told me I could leave after the 45 minutes. That's the whole truth. Now let me go."

Dave wouldn't. "Which building?"

"I told you already, I don't know. He told me to sit low in the back of his filthy-smelling car while he was driving. It was already dark when he started to drive. I went in the backside of a big building. That's all I can remember."

"What did you see inside the building when you opened the door?"

"Just stairs, nothing else. So I sat under the stairs for 45 minutes and when I came out, the alarm went off so I ran."

"So you just sat there and didn't go up the stairs?"

"Yeah, I just sat there, man. Honest to God."

"What size shoes do you wear?"

Peter laughed. "Why, you going to buy me a pair for all this trouble you're putting me through? Make it crocodile skin".

"Don't be funny with me and just answer the question".

"I don't know my shoe size. I just go and buy what ever is cheap and fit my feet".

Dave glanced at Peter's feet. "Where could I find this Caficio?"

"His cousin owns the Mexican bar Margaritas on fifth Street. He mostly hangs around there with his buddies."

"Tell me what he looks like."

Peter grinned. "I just told you he looks Mexican, but I think his mother is Indian. That's all I can tell you".

Dave shook his head. "I need height, weight, hairstyle, eye color, everything you know."

Peter shrugged. "Man, you ask a lot. He's short, about five foot four, has black curly hair and a mustache, about 150 pounds. He has a lot of tattoos."

"What kind of tattoos?"

"Mostly on his hands and arms and a small snake on his neck."

Peter finally got the nod from Dave and re-entered the bar. Dave left, finally feeling like he was getting somewhere. Now he just had to find this 'Caficio'.

Chapter 19

An Inside Job?

At 10:00 am sharp, Diane left her penthouse, determined to take a stress-free day off. Shopping would be just the thing to take her mind off of all the mess that was in her life at the moment. And she had something particular in mind—something she has had her eye on for quite a while. She browsed through several high-end clothing stores just to window shop then, trying on different things and discarding them just as quickly. After a long morning of casual looking, Diane headed for a famous jewelry shop. A man who had been following her the entire time pulled out his small camera and leaned inconspicuously against the display window to watch her. She was fingering several necklaces and chatting with a salesperson. Finally she selected a diamond necklace with an intricate gold chain and signed the receipt for it—all $2,050 of it. Diane then left the store and settled in for a light lunch at a café just two stores down. The man entered the jewelry store and held an intense conversation with the same salesperson. He left quickly when he saw Diane walking away. He tailed her again, until she went into a bank. He waited outside for half an hour until Diane came back out again, and then he resumed his unnoticed trail.

He sat down and noted every detail of Dian's movements including the jewelry shop and the bank visits.

Dave waited in his car directly across from the Margarita Bar, watching passersby disinterestedly until a small, heavily-tattooed man exited the bar, eagerly whistling at a girl passing by, who shot him a dirty glance and kept going. Dave was sure that was Caficio—he perfectly matched the description given to him by Peter. Dave hopped out of the car and jogged across the street to catch up with Caficio.

"Hey, Caficio!"

That man turned, and the leer that had been on his lips when he was looking at the girl was quickly replaced by a hostile glare. He had had his fair share of time with detectives that he could pick them out from a crowd with sometimes-deadly accuracy. His palms were sweating and he tried to seem taller than he was, to appear more threatening to this young, pretentious cop.

"What the hell do you want?" He growled.

Dave flashed his ID. "A couple of days ago, you gave a job to Peter in the Paolo Bar."

Caficio relaxed, and let a surprised look cross his face. "What job? Peter's a liar. There's a reason they call him Con-Man Peter." He snorted derisively. "Like I'm rich enough to throw away a job. I'd do it myself."

Dave took several rather threatening steps forward until mere inches separated the two. "You know which job I'm talking about."

Caficio backed away, wrinkling his nose. "No, I don't. Why you believe him, and not me? Oh you don't believe me because I'm Mexican? Is that it?"

Dave drew a pair of handcuffs from his pocket. "I heard you don't do any jobs yourself. You hire people to do your dirty work. Caficio means 'pimp' in Spanish, doesn't it?"

"Man, I don't care what they call me or why they do."

Dave slid the cuffs back. "If I find out you had something to do with it, I'll make sure you end up behind bars. You understand?"

"Yeah, I understand. But I told you, I didn't give no job to Peter."

"Don't leave town. I will be back. I know where you hang around."

"We will see who the real con man is."

Dave just shook his head and returned to his car. It was a short and uneventful drive back to headquarters where he slid into his chair in his office with a sigh of relief. Sue walked in just minutes later and perched in her usual spot on the edge of his desk.

"What've you got?"

"Well, I narrowed the choices. Is this an inside job or an outside job? That's the question." Sue nodded her agreement, and Dave continued. "I say it's an inside job. Why? Yesterday I got a message from a snitch telling me that a man bragged about an easy money job. So I went to talk to this guy-Peter. He was paid to enter a building at 10:30 pm and told to come out 45 minutes later. He says that when he entered, no alarm sounded, but when he came out, that's when the alarm went off."

"That's a good start." Sue told him. "So how does that make it an inside job?"

"Someone hired Peter as a diversion. Maybe our princess wanted the jewels and the insurance money as well. I'm going to visit her for lunch. I'm going to tell her this information and watch her reaction. I know where she eats lunch every day."

Sue grinned cheekily. "First, she's not *our* princess, she's your princess. Today you know where she eats lunch, tomorrow—where she sleeps."

Dave gave Sue a disgusted look. "Sue, you have a dirty mind."

Sue shrugged innocently. "I'm just telling the truth. Aren't I?"

Dave got up. "Why don't you check for any cars, delivery vans, service vehicles, or taxis that were parked near the building on that day around that time."

Sue knew how far she could push Dave and also knew she was far from the limit. "So I will do all the boring and dirty work and you get to go out to lunch at a nice restaurant?"

Dave smiled. "I know I make most of the sacrifices, but we are a team."

Diane sat in front of Paul's formidable desk; awaiting the reason that Paul had called her in. "How are you progressing with the Hawaii design?"

Diane glanced at her notebook. "The architectural work is almost done and I've sent it to the engineers to complete their part."

"Next week we're scheduled to meet with our Japanese partners to discuss the cost and schedule of this project."

"We shouldn't have any problems meeting that deadline." Diane said confidently.

Paul hesitated, and then plunged forward. "Well, Diane, the question really is, can you handle the meeting alone? I think it would be best if we kept our distance for a while."

Diane looked surprised. "That's fine. Are you ready for lunch?"

Paul shook his head. "No, I'll be having lunch with Christina and my future son-in-law."

A look of mild anger settled on Diane's face. "Well, enjoy." She said stiffly before getting up and walking out. But in the hall, a small triumphant smile lit her face and stayed with her for the rest of the day.

Chapter 20

Surprise Visit

Dave waited in the lobby of the small Italian restaurant, leaning back against the comfortable plush cushions of the benches placed there for that very purpose. After what seemed like a lifetime, the object of his fantasies walked in, looking just as amazing as he had dreamed. Diane saw Dave sitting there, and she couldn't stop the happy smile that spread across her face.

"Waiting for someone, detective?" She asked archly.

"For you." Dave replied simply, his eyes holding hers.

"More questions? Or is this a date?"

Dave shrugged. "May be both."

Diane pouted playfully. "But you didn't ask me out."

"Well, I know you come here for lunch a lot, so I took a chance."

"I have a table reserved, so…" Diane gestured toward the same dim corner they had occupied before and Dave led the way willingly. They sat opposite again, and it took each of them a few minutes to stop staring at one another.

"So what did you want to talk about?" Diane finally asked, stirring her drink with a small spoon.

Dave put aside his attraction for her and focused on the case, looking her straight in the eye. "All the evidence is pointing toward the fact that this is an inside job."

Diane's surprised face was either real or something an actress would have killed to have. "Oh? Don't tell me the security guard did it."

"We're not sure who did it as of right now, but we do know that it is an inside job." Dave watched his suspect carefully, but Diane's face was bland, expressionless as she sipped her drink.

"Give me some more details about your investigation. I want to know all about it."

Dave gave her the edited version. "I talked to a man yesterday who told me that he was paid $200 to go into a building at 10:32 pm and come back out at 11:14 pm. He was supposed to just sit and wait for that time—not do anything else."

Diane's brow lowered. "So what you're telling me is that while he sat there someone from inside the building stole my jewels?"

"That's how we're looking at it."

"Every one of those 200 people in the building is a suspect then."

"Yes, but we can narrow that number easily by checking the whereabouts of the residents at that time. Before we do that, we want to do some more digging on this man." The waiter appeared just then and they both ordered their meals along with a tasty appetizer. "Do you think it could be one of the security guards?" Dave asked the question this time, wanting to see her reaction.

She just smiled.

"You're the detective. I personally don't suspect anyone, but that means it could be anybody. It's your job to find out whom and, if I remember correctly, you're good at solving puzzles."

Diane sent him a little teasing smile as he rolled his eyes in mock irritation. Their orders were served just then, and Dave and Diane let the conversation dwindle away as they enjoyed their meals.

"Dave, you ordered Paul's usual. Don't tell me you checked up on our diets, too?"

Dave laughed, forking more spaghetti into his mouth. "That's not my specialty, I'm afraid." The lunch was soon finished and Diane rose with a regretful look. Dave took the hint from her and rose also, searching for his wallet.

"I feel bad eating free again." He told her as he drew out a bill.

Diane laid a hand on his, shaking her head. "Make it up to me by buying me dinner."

"When?" Dave was already putting the money back in his billfold and returning it to his pocket. Diane laughed. "Next week. I'm leaving Sunday for a business trip to Hawaii. How about next Friday, before I leave?"

"Sounds good to me." Dave entered the date quickly in his planner. "I'll pick you up next Friday at 6:00 pm at your place."

"Any special dress code?"

Dave smiled mysteriously. "Well, we're not going to McDonald's—that's all I can say."

"Oh. Burger King then?"

Dave laughed again. "You just wait and see." He replied, already counting the days.

Chapter 21

Deep Investigation

Sue knocked politely on Dave's desk to get his attention, and then laid a folder of papers in front of him when he looked up. "Look what I got. I was looking for leads on any unknown cars parked at the location. An old lady who lives a block from the building said that a person with dark hair was driving in that area about 11:00 pm—just going around and around the block. The car was dirty and dark and she never saw them park. The lady had lost her cat so she was outside looking for it when she noticed the car circling. She wrote down the license plate number." Sue pointed to the paper, which held all the information.

"Did you run the plate?"

"Yes. It belongs to Carlos Fernandez. He's been under suspicion many times, usually just in petty robberies, but we've never been able to pin anything on him."

Dave thought for a few seconds. "It could be that guy I checked yesterday. Any parking tickets or other violations?"

"He has quite a few of both."

"Good. We have enough to pick him up for questioning." Dave filed the information away in a lower file cabinet beside his desk. "Good work, Sue. Tell our boys to pick him up tomorrow morning and bring him here for questioning."

"So what happened with the princess?" Sue asked with a smile.

Dave refused to take the bait. "Her facial reaction was normal. But I did find out that she is going to Hawaii on Sunday for a week, on business. And I want to check on the last time she went to Hawaii. It's a possibility that she took the jewels a while ago to Hawaii and left them there."

"So you're going to follow her to Hawaii? Sounds like a good plan. The chief will love this idea."

"You're just jealous because you're married and missing those single days." Dave grinned triumphantly as Sue just shrugged, bereft of a fitting comeback.

The next morning, Caficio sat at the interrogation table, inspecting his fingernails with a studious air. Dave and Sue entered and took their seats across the table from him.

"Hello, Mr. Fernandez." Dave said. "You remember me, don't you?"

Caficio grinned. "Yeah, I have a good memory for ugly faces."

Dave shrugged calmly. "You want to be smart, go ahead. It won't get you anywhere. Just tell us the truth and we'll let you go."

"What do you want to know?"

"An honest answer to the same question I asked you the other day. Who gave you the job?"

"I don't know a name. A woman called me a few days ago and gave me the job."

"No name? What does she look like?"

Caficio sent a disgusted glare Dave's way. "Man, I never saw her, she called my cell phone."

"How much did she pay you?"

"One grand."

"How did you get the money?"

"A bicycle delivery boy gave it to me with the key."

"Did you recognize the delivery boy?"

"No, man, there are hundreds of them." A light shone suddenly in Caficio's face. "Hey, I remember something! She said to call her Medea or Media or something like that."

"Medea?" Sue asked.

"Yeah, but it was probably a fake name."

Sue smiled. "You can bet on that. Medea is a character in Greek mythology. She was a scorned woman who sought vengeance through magic and trickery."

Caficio looked bored. "Whatever. I only heard her voice on the phone."

"What did her voice sound like?"

"Pushy, demanding."

"How many times did she call you?"

Caficio squinted into the light as he thought. "I think three times."

"You being straight with us?" Dave asked suspiciously. "You lied the last time."

"Man, this is the full truth."

"How did she get your number?"

"I don't know. I put ads in local papers about small moving jobs, stuff like that. Maybe she got it from there."

"So explain to me what she wanted you to do?"

"She said at 10:30 pm sharp I was to open the back door of the Rittman building and stay inside for 45 minutes—then come back out and run away."

"Did you ask her why?"

"Yeah, but she said, 'Do you want this job or not?'"

Sue gestured swiftly to Dave and pulled him aside. "Maybe we should call our princess and let him listen to her voice. If it's her, he might be able to identify it."

"Good thinking." Dave set up the speakerphone on the table. "I'm going to talk to a woman right now. Don't say anything, just listen. Understand?" Caficio nodded and Dave dialed Diane's number. Diane's voice crackled loud and clear from the speaker.

"Hello?"

"Diane, this is Dave Merko. How are you doing today?"

"I'm fine. Don't tell me you're canceling our dinner appointment."

"No, nothing like that." Dave glanced at Caficio and that man just shrugged, his face signaling a complete blank.

"More questions? Or did you find the jewels?"

"I made a reservation at a really great seafood restaurant." Dave told her, ignoring her questions. "Do you like seafood?"

"I love seafood."

"Great. I'll see you at six tomorrow."

"Okay. See you tomorrow." Dave hung up.

Caficio laughed. "That's your girlfriend, man?"

"Never mind that. Did you recognize the voice?"

"I don't know. May be she was disguising it the other night, making it sound really rough. I don't know. I am not a voice expert".

"Why did you give the job to Peter?"

"I was having my doubts about the job. I didn't want to get involved in something I don't know enough about. So I gave it to Peter."

"Well, I'll let you go for now, but don't leave town. You know I can arrest you anytime, with those parking tickets."

"So, if I pay them, you won't arrest me?"

Dave frowned. "Don't play games with me. I'll find a way to get you."

Chapter 22

Love or Serious Investigation?

Dave knocked on the chief's door and waited until Ron called him in. The chief looked up as he sat in front of him. "You have good news about the case?"

"Yes. It's coming together quite interestingly. We questioned a guy today who was hired by a woman to enter the Rittman building at 10:32 pm and hide there for 45 minutes. He never saw the woman, just heard her voice. My suspicion is that the woman was Diane Taylor."

Ron looked at Dave for a long moment. "I told you before to be very careful about accusing Rittman or Taylor. So why her?"

"She's the only one who knows about the jewels other than Rittman. She's the only one who will benefit from this. The safe is in her penthouse. I looked at the jewelry receipts and appraisal—they are, on average worth $800,000 each. They aren't things you can just sell on the streets. I strongly believe she took them to get insurance money. I'm sure of it."

Ron, who had great confidence in his top detective's intuition, paused for a minute, weighing the information. "So what's your next step?"

"The only way to get a break is by getting closer to her and observing her actions or getting her to admit it. I met Miss Taylor a couple of times and she asked me to buy her dinner tomorrow night. She seems to like my company and I want to take advantage of it. I want her to keep liking me."

"Sounds like a James Bond movie. Be careful. Powerful people are on her side."

"I'll be legal, prudent, and savvy." Dave assured him. "She told me that she'll be leaving for Hawaii on Sunday on a business trip for a week. I'm seriously thinking of following her. During my dinner should I give her the impression that I may want to join her?"

Ron looked skeptical. "Follow her to Hawaii? You're not interested in her and this is strictly business?"

Dave smiled. "I won't play *that* part of James Bond."

Ron hesitated still. "I'll have to think about it. Call me after your dinner. I'll make my decision then." Dave nodded gratefully and practically bounded out the door before Ron could change his mind.

Dave pulled up in front of Diane's penthouse at exactly 5:59 pm according to his new watch. Diane was waiting outside the front door with an eager expression she was trying hard to mask. She eyed his sleek sports car as he walked around the car to open the passenger door for her.

"You look great." He told her, noticing the exquisite necklace that adorned her throat.

"Thanks." Diane smiled almost shyly as she slid into the seat. Dave re-entered his side and started the car with a rev of the humming engine. "Nice car. I feel like I just stepped into a girl trap."

Dave glanced at her. "I'd say you have." They both laughed as Dave sped away. A popular song came on the radio and Diane reached quickly to turn it up.

"Oh, I love this song!" She exclaimed excitedly.

Dave turned it a little louder. "Me too. Just one more thing we have in common." They enjoyed a companionable silence until Dave parked at the seafood restaurant. They were soon seated at an intimate table for two overlooking a splendid view of the mountains and a fiery sunset that was cleansing the sky with its burning hues. Diane watched it wistfully.

"Just look at the sunset…it's beautiful. You have good taste in restaurants." She took a deep breath. "It's been a long time since I've felt this happy."

"You mean after the break-in?"

"No, I'd say it started two or three months before that."

"Does it have to do with love, money, or health?" Dave quizzed, wanting to know the answer. Diane looked away. "A little bit of two of those, but I won't tell you which two."

"Okay. That's fine." Dave opened his menu and Diane followed suit. "To me, this is the best seafood place in town," he told her.

"So what do you suggest?"

"For an appetizer, try the raw oysters." Dave's eyes twinkled as he watched for her reaction. "They're good for your sex life."

Diane laughed. "Well, I'm not planning to have sex tonight."

Dave shrugged as if it were entirely her loss. "Try the halibut for the main course. It's really very good."

"Okay, then, I will take your advice." Diane did as she said and ordered the halibut in the creamy lemon sauce with a side of coleslaw, and Dave ordered the same. Their food arrived soon enough, and Dave took the plunge into deeper conversation.

"Can I ask you a personal question, Diane?"

Diane looked surprised. "How personal?"

"Why is a smart and beautiful woman like you not married?"

"There are really two reasons. I haven't found the right man and I'm too busy with my work."

"So tell me about the right man."

Diane smiled. "Hmm....tall, handsome, rich, kind, and cheerful."

Dave laughed. "So you're never getting married."

Diane shrugged in partial agreement. "I don't really have physical or personality requirements. I'll just know, inside, that he's the right one for me."

"So, no stereotype such as tall, blue eyes, brown hair, handsome?"

Dave pretended he wasn't describing himself and waited quite seriously for her answer.

Diane rolled her eyes. "Well, some, yes."

"Then I can easily be that guy." Dave laughed and was glad to see Diane took his joke and chuckled too. They held gazes for a brief, charged second and then Diane broke the silence.

"So tell me why you are not married?"

"How do you know I am not married?'

"Come on Dave. Your looks tell all. You don't wear a ring, the way you dress and the way you look at girls and your charming and flattering behavior. Do I look like an eighteen year old girl?'

"Okay, you got me. First, I don't have the time. I'm so busy chasing criminals and taking on more cases that my demanding chief hands over, that it leaves me no time to socialize."

"So this is not social? Just investigation?"

"Wait a minute, you ask me a question and then pick on me?"

"So answer the question. Is this social or part of your investigation?"

"If I remember correctly, you actually asked me to buy you dinner."

"Do you just buy dinner for whoever asks you?"

"It depends. I should have a reason and I must like the company I'm entertaining."

"So which category am I in?"

Dave looked deep into her eyes. "You're in both, so I couldn't refuse."

"So you like the company and what is the reason?"

"Get to know you better."

He hesitated, realizing that now was as good a time as any to bring up the subject of Hawaii. "So why are you going to Hawaii?"

"I'm designing a hotel and apartment complex on the big island. Paul and a Japanese company are partners. I'm going there to review the architectural plans with them. Why do you want to know?"

"I've never been to Hawaii. I'd love to go there some day. Tell me about it."

"Oh, it's a beautiful place. Nice weather, clean beaches, and amazing seafood. Our company has a hotel right on the beachfront."

Dave pushed a little bit. "How about inviting me next time you go?" He teased, feigning nonchalance. "Well, why don't you come this time?"

"Really?" Diane nodded.

"I'd have to get my boss's permission to take a vacation because I'm still working on this case." "That's the perfect opportunity." Diane pointed out.

"What do you mean?"

"You said it looks like an inside job. Tell your boss that you need to check on me. So take it as an official trip. You don't have to spend a dime. The police department will pay all".

Dave couldn't believe his luck. "You think he'll buy that?"

"Why not? I easily fall into the motive category because I'm the only one who gains from the insurance. Right?" Dave gave her a closer look. "You're serious, aren't you?"

"The invitation or the motive?" Diane laughed. "I'll talk to my boss." Dave promised, feeling as if he were on cloud nine.

Chapter 23

Hawaii

The couple sat in Dave's car in front of Diane's apartment building. Dave reached for Diane's hand and rubbed his thumb gently across the top of it, feeling its softness and smallness. The night had been wonderful—the food delicious, the conversation titillating, the wine bubbly, and the glances intoxicating. Diane couldn't believe that after such a short time, she had fallen so hard for this man. Dave was much in the same boat. He loved the sound of her voice, the expressions she used, and the way her dark eyes danced when he teased her. He decided to go ahead and broach the Hawaii subject again.

"So, if my boss decides to let me go on a holiday or investigation, how do I contact you in Hawaii?" Diane removed her hand from his rather reluctantly and retrieved a slip of paper and a pen from her purse. She jotted down a number and slid it into Dave's pocket herself.

"Here's my number and address. Thanks for the dinner. I really enjoyed it." Her eyes spoke volumes as they met his.

Dave smiled. "The food or the company?"

"The food for sure; the company remains questionable." Diane laughed to show she was joking and slid out of the car. With one last smile, she closed the door softly and Dave sped off with a friendly honk.

Dave pulled his cell phone from his hip pocket and dialed Ron Matthews' number.

"Hello?"

"Ron, this is Dave."

Ron's voice sounded angry. "I'm in bed. What is so urgent for you to call me at this time of night? I was sleeping and you put me up. This had better be good."

"She's invited me to go to Hawaii assuming I'll get permission from you to follow and investigate her. She who? What are you talking about?

"Sir I am talking about the jewels robbery and Diane Taylor".

Ron was silent for a few seconds. "Is she trying to be smart or falling in love with you or are you falling in love with her or both?"

Dave's heart clenched. He dearly hoped that it was the latter, but he couldn't admit such a thing to his boss, and certainly not in this situation. "I'm almost certain she has a lot to do with it. By going to Hawaii, I should be able to break the case wide open."

Ron was silent again; this time so long that Dave thought he had fallen asleep. Finally he answered. "When were you planning to leave?"

Dave tapped the wheel joyfully. "Monday."

"Well, I hope you know what you're doing. Okay, get the ticket. I'll approve it. But if I see big restaurant bills you'll be the one paying."

"You won't see any of that, sir. Thank you." Dave hung up,

unable to keep a broad smile off his face. He dialed again.

"Hello?"

"Hi, Sue, it's Dave. I hope I didn't catch you in bed like Ron."

Sue laughed. "No, we're just making love on the couch."

Dave's smile disappeared quickly. "Sorry I asked. Now, get this: I'll be going to Hawaii on Monday. This will be an opportunity for you to go to Diane's penthouse and give that place a thorough search. Also check her friend Chandra's apartment too. You may have to get Mr. Rittman's okay and may have to get search warrants. Check with Ron"

Sue felt a twinge of jealousy. "You get to go to Hawaii and I just get to go check out her apartment? Sounds like a convenient set up to me. Does Ron know about this?"

"I just got off the phone with him."

"And he said go ahead, my most brilliant detective?" You could hear the smirk coming from Sue's end of the line.

"Sue, why are you so angry about this? You know it is an inside job and who's going to benefit from this robbery."

"Yes, I know who is going to benefit from this robbery. You are. You get a free trip and I don't want to say what else."

"Wish me luck."

"Luck for what? Catching her or…" Sue let the sentence trail off, but Dave had no doubts about what she was implying. He laughed and hung up.

Chapter 24

Perfect Landing

The Honolulu airport was set in the midst of lush tropical suburban jungle. Palm trees and bright tropical flowers liberally dotted the surrounding area amid towering skyscrapers and roaring traffic. The air was balmy and the breeze warmed Dave's face as he exited the terminal and hailed a cab. He handed a slip of paper to the cabbie and sat back against the worn leather seat, enjoying the beautiful scenery. The cab soon arrived in front of a large hotel with the name "Rittman Suites" emblazoned in gold across the front. Dave paid the cab driver and carried his bags inside. He found a house phone and dialed Diane's number.

Diane had just slipped into a short silky dress when the phone rang. She picked it up, already trembling with anticipation. "Hello?"

"This is Dave. I'm here."

"You're kidding."

"Really, I am in the lobby."

"Okay, come on up." Diane hung up, and mentally gave herself a good talking to regarding the odd flutters in her stomach and shivers down her spine that had burst out upon hearing the deep voice on the other end of the line. The knock on her door just minutes later startled her, and she pressed a hand to her pounding heart as she hurried to open the door. Dave was standing there, just as handsome as ever, with a travel bag in his hand.

"Are you on vacation or official trip"?

Dave said with a smile.

"I am on an official and investigation trip".

"How did you manage to get approval?"

Diane wondered as she let him in.

"You gave me the answer."

"You really used that? And you're going to follow me everywhere I go? And what happens if you don't find anything?"

"Let me worry about that. You just show me Hawaii and let me have a good time. I should have taken this vacation a long time ago."

Diane poured him a glass of water solicitously. "Have you booked a hotel?"

"I didn't have the time." Dave admitted. "I was hoping you could get me a room here, since you have such influence." He was teasing again, but Diane didn't mind.

"They're fully booked because of a big convention. I have two bedrooms, though. You could use one tonight. I'll get you one tomorrow."

"You trust me that much?"

Diane arched an eyebrow and put her hands on her hips. "Let me make this crystal clear: you sleep in your room and I sleep in mine. This has nothing to do with trust and everything to do with friendship and help."

Dave shrugged obligingly. "Fair enough." He took a short tour around the room and ended at the window with the view of the white beach and jewel-toned waves. "This is a palace. Nice to be rich."

Diane laughed. "I'm sure you will be very comfortable."

Dave looked pointedly at the expensive furnishings and state-of-the-art appliances. "Comfortable wasn't quite the word I had in mind."

Diane pointed toward a room. "That's your room. You're lucky you caught me, actually. I was just about to go for a walk on the beach and then to dinner. Are you ready to come?"

"Well, since it seems you've made up your mind that you will be enjoying my company, how can I refuse?"

Diane laughed. "Well, let's go then.

Dave and Diane walked along the beach, hand in hand, deep in conversation. The waves crashed and rolled along the sand, foaming at their feet, and then retreating back to their sea. The moonlight glittered on the ocean, leaving a trail of stardust from the shore to the horizon. The night was peaceful, serene. A camera clicked. The same man who had followed Diane in Seattle was there, lens and shutter at the ready.

Oblivious to their silent stalker, Dave and Diane strolled into a luxury restaurant that had a one-of-a-kind view of the sea. A waiter who was obviously familiar with Diane seated them quickly, paying them as many compliments as he could fit in three sentences. Dave looked around when they were seated.

"Do you always eat at places like this?"

Diane tried to see the place she took for granted through Dave's middle-class eyes. "I guess I've been spoiled by Paul. We always came here for dinner at least three or four times each trip." "You're a spoiled brat!" Dave observed half-teasingly.

"Once you're used to a high standard of living, it's hard to settle for less." Diane admitted. "Just like a drug addict. That's why the rich always want to be richer."

"Well, you'll be richer once you get the money from the insurance."

"You forgot your promise?"

"What promise?"

"That you will get my jewels back."

Dave laughed. The maitre'd brought the food just then and the two spent the rest of the meal in idle chitchat. Their waiter brought the check eventually and Diane waved off Dave's attempts to pay. She took out cash—and not just a few bills, but a whole fistful of green—and counted out the correct amount, adding in a generous tip. Dave's eyes widened as he saw the amount of cash Diane had.

"Aren't credit cards safer?"

"Is that a detective question?"

"No."

Diane smiled mysteriously as she returned the bills to her wallet. "Then I don't have to answer.

Chapter 25

Love and Investigation?

The morning sun streamed in through the windows, falling across Dave's eyes and brightening the back of his eyelids. He groaned and threw an arm over his face, rolling back onto his pillow. He finally got up and staggered to the window where he felt much more revived after a few minutes of watching the seascape. He pulled on a t-shirt and walked out to the living room—it was empty. A note was propped on the coffee table, covered with flowing script. He picked it up and read it, then smiled.

Don't look for a hotel. You are welcome to stay with me—I DO like your company. See you at four p.m.   Diane

Dave quickly showered and dressed in a pair of tailored jeans and a button-down blue collared shirt. He slipped a gold chain around his neck and headed down to the hotel reception desk. The receptionist greeted him warmly as he approached. He removed the gold chain and placed it on the desk.

"Could you please put this in the hotel safe with Miss Diane Taylor's items? We're staying together in her penthouse."

"I'm aware of that sir, but Miss Taylor never brings anything to keep in our safe."

"Hmmm…well, in that case, I'll just wear it." Dave shrugged off her objections and exited the hotel. He walked until he reached a bank. He showed his ID to a security guard and quietly asked for a manager.

"What's the problem, officer?" The manager, resplendent in a pin-striped suit, had visions of lawsuits in his head as he led Dave toward a quiet corner.

"No problem, but I would like to check if you have an account under the name Diane Taylor."

"Come to my office, let me check." Dave followed the manager into a well-furnished office where he punched in a few keys on the computer and typed in Diane's name. "Nothing. No accounts under the name Diane Taylor."

"Not even a safety deposit box?"

"Nothing whatsoever."

Dave thanked the man for his time and continued his search. But it turned up fruitless; every other bank within fifteen miles contained managers who shook their heads and told him that Miss Taylor had "no account or safety deposit box registered." Dave finally went back to the hotel suite to wait for Diane. He was watching the television when Diane returned.

"How was your day?" He asked, feeling strangely marital towards the woman who had plopped down on the couch next to him.

"Good! It was very productive. Thanks for asking. I'm hungry; let's go get something to eat. I'll be ready in ten minutes."

Dave nodded and Diane slipped into her bedroom to change out of her elegant pantsuit.

Dave and Diane entered the City Lights nightclub, arm in arm and laughing at something Dave had said. The man with the camera followed at a safe distance, intermittently snapping pictures. They spent most of the night at the club, and then made their way back to the hotel, fingers intertwined and looking more disheveled than they had been when they had walked in. They were lounging on the couch in the penthouse at midnight, sipping on drinks and talking about their night.

"Tomorrow I'll be going to work at the same time I did today. You just relax and have fun and I'll see you at four again." Diane informed Dave.

"Why don't you take a day off for me?" Dave put on his best pleading face.

Diane bit back a smile, trying not to encourage him. "Dave, this is an important project. People will be waiting for me. I just can't."

Dave's face dropped. "Well, I'll take a tour bus and see the island by myself then."

Diane stood and stretched. "Well, that sounds like a good idea." She yawned widely. "I'm getting tired. I think I'll turn in for the night."

"Good night, Diane." Dave watched her close her bedroom door, doubting that he would get much sleep tonight being so close to her.

The next morning Dave was in the same spot he was the night before, this time with a steaming cup of coffee in his hand. He was deep in thought, almost forgetting about the scalding temperature of the liquid when he jumped up from the couch. He set the cup on the coffee table, absentmindedly wiping a few drops off his hand as he gazed at Diane's partially opened door. He walked into her bedroom and began to poke around, opening drawers and looking between the mattresses. He found the handbag she had carried the night before and sifted through the contents. He found a small, palm-sized manila envelope with the words "Wells Fargo Bank, 110 Broadway Seattle" written on it in Diane's flowing handwriting. He opened the envelope and slid the contents—a solid key—into his palm. Without hesitation, he retrieved a small box from his room and pressed the key into the piece of clay that lay inside. He slipped the box—with the key impression safely inside—back into his travel case and then made sure the room looked undisturbed before he carefully pulled the door to the position it had been in before.

Dave checked his watch again for the hundredth time as he waited outside the hotel for Diane to show up. Just when he was ready to go back inside, Diane appeared around the corner. She greeted him with a smile, which he gladly returned.

"So what did you do today?" Diane asked as they began walking toward the beach.

"I saw the whole island in five hours."

"So you're really leaving tomorrow?"

"Yes. I have to be in court on Friday."

"What time is your flight?"

"Four pm."

"I can leave early tomorrow and take you to the airport."

"Thanks. I'd appreciate that." Dave glanced at Diane. "It's my last night here. Let's spend some time at the beach. I brought a blanket." He held up the colorful fabric.

"Okay. I'm game."

Diane and Dave sat on the blanket, watching the sun set. The rays shot the ocean with sparkles of pink, red, and yellow. Above them, the stars had begun to twinkle in an indigo sky lit with a brilliant moon, shedding light on the picnic dinner they were feasting on. They shared conversation in low, intimate tones, laughing softly at the appropriate moments. Dave slid a finger down Diane's cheek and leaned in for a kiss. Diane responded eagerly, kissing him ardently. They lay back on the blanket, entwined in each other's arms. The man with the camera captured it all on film.

Dave woke the next morning in Diane's bed, pulling the blankets around him in a belated sense of modesty. The other side of the bed was empty, save for a note on Diane's pillow. The paper contained only a hurried drawing of a heart. Dave jumped out of bed, wrapped himself with a bed sheet and headed to the bathroom, where he showered and then pulled his clothes on. He dug through his things until he found his cell phone, and then dialed Ron's number.

"Hey, Ron, this is Dave."

"Did you get what you said or did you just have fun on department money?"

Dave looked guiltily at the bedroom door. "It's serious work, chief. I found a safety deposit key in her handbag."

"What does that mean?"

"If she kept her jewels in the safe, why should she need a bank safety deposit box? She has a safe in her penthouse."

"That makes sense. You got the key?"

"I made an imprint. I want you to get a search warrant for the bank box."

"Which bank is it?"

"Wells Fargo on 110 Broadway. I'll be there first thing

Saturday."

"Okay, I'll work on it. No guarantees, but I'll try my best."

Dave lie on the beach, sun bathing. A shadow fell over him and he squinted into the sun to find Diane smiling down on him.

"You want to catch every ray of sun before you leave?"

"When you live in Seattle, you better get sun whenever you get an opportunity. Here I am I Hawaii and I better get as much as sun I can." Dave replied. Diane sat beside him and pulled off her heels, rubbing her feet into the sand. "Rough day?" He asked kindly. Diane just curled up beside him, needing human comfort. Dave kissed her on the forehead.

Chapter 26

Washington

Diane and Dave sat quietly as the limo took them to the airport. Diane watched the scenery flash by and finally asked the question that had been plaguing her for quite some time.

"So what are you going to tell your boss?"

"I'll think of something believable on the plane."

Diane smiled. "Don't make it too believable."

"Why not?"

"When I come back to Seattle they might arrest me."

"So tell me where you hid them." Dave changed gears quickly and dangerously.

"I'm confused as to what you're referring to." Diane replied calmly, her face stoic.

Dave looked right into her eyes, his expression serious. "Where? In a bank safety deposit box?"

Diane's eyes filled with tears and she blinked rapidly to dissipate them. "You are...I don't know." The limo arrived at the airport. Dave got out. Diane stayed inside. "Have a good flight home," she told him, her voice emotionless.

He couldn't believe that this was goodbye after the passionate, emotional week they had just spent together. He reluctantly bid her farewell and watched as the limo pulled away carrying the woman he ached for back to the hotel, back to the room where they had consummated their attraction for each other. He walked into the terminal without looking back.

Diane rummaged in her purse until she found the small envelope. She pulled the key out, and then frowned. She sniffed it, and then held it close to examine it. A tiny, almost unnoticeable piece of clay was stuck to one of the teeth. Dave had done exactly what she'd predicted he would. She smiled triumphantly.

Dave, Ron, and the insurance investigator Mike followed rapidly the bank manager at Wells Fargo rapidly down a long stainless steel corridor. The manger glanced back at Ron.

"This box was rented only a few days ago." She told them.

"How many, exactly?" Dave wanted to know.

"Ten days ago."

Dave looked pointedly at Ron. "That's four days <u>after</u> the robbery."

The group entered a large room, its walls lined with boxes, each numbered. The manager pulled a small silver box from the wall and placed it on a table. Dave pulled the copy of the key that he had made, and opened the box. Inside were one diamond necklace and a credit card receipt. All three men looked puzzled. Mike picked up both items and examined the necklace closely.

"This necklace isn't part of the insured jewels. This is a cheap necklace. According to the receipt, it cost only $2,050."

Ron turned to the manager, his face angry. "Thank you for

your time and cooperation."

Mike was still turning the necklace over in his hands. "This must be the necklace one of our agents saw Miss Taylor buying." The manager escorted them back out and Ron waited until they were in the car to talk to Dave.

"Dave, I know you tried your best. I think it's time to turn our attention to other suspects."

Dave looked down at his hands. "I'm really sorry, except I'm certain she did it."

"Sue checked the penthouse inch by inch and found nothing suspicious. The search should have given us some clue. The size ten footprint is still there."

"But the guy told us that a lady hired him."

"Someone could have disguised their voice." Ron pointed out. "We can't be sure that it was Miss Taylor. So, my conclusion is that we are wasting our time on the wrong person."

Dave gave in to the higher authority. "If you strongly believe that, I'll start looking at other suspects."

Diane walked into Paul's office just a few hours after she returned from Hawaii. Paul looked at her rather unhappily. "Come in Diane. Close the door behind you." Diane did as she was told, her face set in lines of resignation.

"I've made an important decision. I never thought in my life that I would have to make such a difficult one as I have today, but the situation I'm in demands it." Paul unlocked a drawer and pulled out a file folder, which he handed to Diane. Diane opened it. Inside were photos of her and Dave entering the night club, walking into the restaurant, kissing on the beach—Diane shut the folder.

"So you had a spy checking up on me?" She asked angrily.

"No, the insurance investigator took these. They sent them to me. But the pictures are not the real issue here."

"What is the real issue, then?"

"I need you to find another job."

Diane paused. "I knew we would come to an end, but this is a little harsher than I expected. If I leave, I'm not going empty-handed."

"You'll be given a year's salary and a year with the company's benefits."

"That's not what I was thinking." Diane informed him. "I want the penthouse and the apartment in Hawaii. I spent six years with you—you owe it to me."

"That's a lot to ask." They were both quiet. "I lost more than a million dollars in cash in that safe. I kept it there for our future. Now you'll get the insurance money for your jewels, but I won't get my cash. I didn't want to claim that money with the insurance because questions will be raised like—'Why so much cash?' The IRS, my family, the press, the insurance—they would all be after me with questions."

Diane shrugged. "It's too bad about your money, but I have to look after myself. The penthouse and apartment in Hawaii are just a drop in the bucket for you, but they are a necessity to me. Suppose I expose our relationship? That would cost you far more than a bit of real estate. And I don't have to mention what it would do to your family and your reputation. It's your call."

Paul's face reddened and he pushed his hands through his hair, making it stand on end. His hands were shaking as he folded them in his lap. He thought for a few minutes. "Okay. You can have them as long as you make no other demands or threats of exposure."

"I'll agree to that. I give you my solemn word. I just need to know why. I was living on dreams, on spending my life with you. I, at least, deserve part of that dream."

Paul hung his head, unable to say anything. He put his face in his hands and waved toward the door, signaling that the conversation was over. "I'll instruct my lawyer to transfer the penthouse and the Hawaii apartment to you."

Diane paused at the door. "Thank you. I'll turn in my resignation today." She turned and walked out, leaving behind no regrets.

Chapter 27

What is the Next Step?

Sue walked into Dave's office with a cunning smile. "So, Romeo how was the honeymoon? You couldn't catch her, but you did have fun, right?"

Dave couldn't stop the sunshine that spread across his face. "How did you know?"

"I can see it in your face and in hers when she looks at you."

Dave tried hard to get back to business. "Do you have any other leads we can work on?"

Ron burst right in, a thundercloud looming on his brow. He pointed at Dave menacingly. "My office. Now, Mr. Bond." Dave didn't try to waste words; he simply followed Ron to his office quietly. In Ron's office, Ron took a seat behind his desk and tossed a bunch of photos in front of Dave. There were the pictures of him and Diane on the beach kissing. Ron watched Dave closely with obvious annoyance in his eyes.

"Explain. You can lie and say these aren't yours, but we both know how far that will get you."

"Well, uh…it's me and her…" Dave tried to think of an explanation.

"You went to Hawaii to investigate her, not..." Ron fairly spluttered in rage as he gestured towards the photos scattered across his desk.

"It just happened. I brought the bank deposit information back for you." Dave said desperately, hoping for any way out. "I wasn't there just to play games."

Ron shook his head. "But you did exactly that. I hope this doesn't get into the hands of the press. You are officially off this case and I'm suspending you for a week without pay."

Dave stood reluctantly. "I am sorry, sir. I disagree, but I understand."

Ron waved him away wearily. "Put your badge and gun on my desk and get out of here."

The man situated across the street from the Wells Fargo Bank with his camera seemed to be thoroughly engrossed in his newspaper. He flipped a page, leaning casually against the wall. His next move was so smooth and quick that people wondered what had happened. He tossed the paper into a trashcan, and was on his way across the street before any one could blink. Diane had just left the bank with what was obviously the diamond necklace she bought a few weeks ago now hanging around her neck. The man looked clearly disappointed when she hailed a cab and drove away toward her apartment building.

Diane approached the security guard station in her apartment building lobby. Trevor was on duty and looked sharply at attention as she neared.

"Trevor, I'll be gone for a few days to Hawaii. Could you please make sure that you collect all my letters and packages from my mailbox and put them in my closet in the storage area? Here is the key to my storage and this is my mailbox key. I don't want anyone to know I'm out of town."

Trevor smiled helpfully, enjoying the view as usual. "No problem, Miss Taylor."

Dave waited in the lobby of the Italian restaurant at noon, hoping that Diane would show up as she usually did. The manager walked over.

"Table for one, sir?"

"Thanks, but I'm waiting for Diane Taylor." "I'm sorry, sir, but she was here yesterday and told me she will be gone for a few days." Dave was surprised. "Did she tell you where?"

"No, sir." Dave thanked him again and made his way quickly over to the apartment building and to the receptionist seated behind the desk.

"Is Diane Taylor available?"

The girl's expression showed immediate sadness. "I'm sorry, but she resigned from her job yesterday and went to Hawaii."

That answer was certainly not the one Dave had expected. "Resigned? Could I see Mr. Rittman?"

She shook her head again. "I'm afraid he went to City Hall for a meeting. He won't be back until tomorrow."

"Thanks anyway." Dave sighed with frustration and left. Then an idea dawned and he picked up the pace towards home.

At home, Dave threw clothes and toiletries into his travel suitcase and he called a popular travel agency. He made the arrangements and then took a cab to SeaTac Airport where he boarded a large passenger jet—destination: Hawaii.

Chapter 28

Dave in Love?

Dave stood wearily in front of the hotel desk, dropping his bag at his feet. "May I use the phone?"

"Certainly, sir. And welcome back." The clerk had a penchant for remembering faces, and he was paid to do so.

"Thanks." Dave dialed Diane's hotel penthouse number—no answer. He tried Diane's cell phone and got the same result. Where could she be at nine o'clock at night? "Have you seen Miss Taylor?" He finally asked.

The clerk scratched his head. "Yes, I remember seeing her this evening going out to the beach. I haven't seen her since."

Dave hoisted his bag onto the counter. "Would you keep this for me? I'll be back soon." And he was off like a shot in the direction of the beach, his energy renewed. At a fast pace that could almost be called a jog, Dave perused the bars and restaurants along the shoreline with no luck. On a whim, he decided to try a little café tucked away from the high-end businesses towards a smaller part of the beach. There sat Diane, watching the surf crash into the sand. Dave appeared at her side and she glanced up to see who it was. Her face twisted into a mask of confusion and hurt. Dave pulled out a chair and sat down, taking her hands in his.

"We have to stop meeting like this," he said softly. Diane didn't reply, a shocked expression still on her face. "You're supposed to ask, 'What are you doing here?'" Dave prompted.

"What are you doing here?" Diane asked flatly, pulling her hands away and picking up her cup of coffee again.

"I came to Hawaii to see you. You told me that I was welcome any time."

Diane finally looked at him, angry now. "Tell me the truth, Dave."

"I went to see you at your office and was told that you quit and had come here. And considering I'm on a one week suspension for kissing you, I had plenty of time to come find you."

Diane looked slightly mollified. "How did they know you kissed me?"

"The insurance investigator is quite the photographer." Dave told her wryly.

A small smile peeked out. "Paul showed me the same pictures."

Dave frowned. "So he forced you to quit?"

"Not exactly. He told me to look for a new job, so I beat him to the punch and just quit." Diane was quiet again, wrapping her fingers around her mug. "I don't know if I even want to talk to you."

Dave made sure she was looking him in the eye and asked, "Are you happy to see me or not?"

Diane paused. "Why are you here? Tell me the truth."

"I told you the truth! I enjoy being with you and I was a little concerned after I heard you lost your job. I knew this is where you would come and I thought you might need me."

"You're concerned about me? That's the biggest joke I've heard in a long time." She tried to laugh, but she couldn't force much more than a squeak past the sudden lump in her throat.

For the first time, Dave looked angry. "How am I supposed to prove that? You can't just believe me?"

"You said that you were suspended for one week. Well, you've got this week to prove you care or to tell me the truth."

Dave smiled. "You want me to find a room or stay at your place?"

"You can stay with me, but you'll be in your own room again." She managed another small smile to show she wasn't as upset as she pretended she was.

The next morning Dave found Diane in the living room, reading a mystery novel. She looked peaceful and serene, the worried lines from last night erased by a hard sleep. She greeted him with a smile.

"Good morning. How did you sleep?"

Dave rubbed his hands over his hair and down his face. "I had a scotch. That helped." There was a knock on the door.

"I ordered breakfast." Diane informed him cheerfully as she rose to answer it. She let in two bellboys, each with a rolling cart full of food. Diane tipped them each generously from her full wallet and they left quickly, their eyes wide at the amount of cash placed in their palms. She brought each tray over to the coffee table where Dave was sitting and placed one in front of him and the other in front of her. She tucked her legs under her gracefully and sat on the floor to eat.

"So are you going to look for work?" Dave asked between bites of the delicious food.

"A Japanese builder wanted me to design a building for him about three months ago. I'm considering to contacting him to take the offer."

They were silent, each enjoying the feast, until Dave suddenly thought of something. "You resigned, and you still get to use this suite?"

Diane's expression dimmed. "Yes, it was given to me as a bonus."

"So how long are you going to stay?"

Diane rolled her eyes. "Dave, stop asking so many questions and eat your breakfast." Dave did as he was told, but Diane had a harder time. Her eyes filled with tears and she pressed her lips together to stop the emotions. "Why are you here?" She finally burst out. "Is this your entertainment?"

Dave froze, a bite halfway to his mouth. "What do you mean?"

"Do you trust anyone, ever?"

Dave was silent, not sure how to answer, so Diane plunged ahead. "Last time when I invited you to stay here, you went into my room when I was gone and took an imprint of my safety deposit key." Dave's face dropped. "Then you went to the bank and opened the box to see if the jewels were there. How can I possibly trust you now?"

Dave felt ashamed. "I had to take something with me to satisfy my boss. I found the key and I used it. This time I'm on my own. I was worried about you when I heard that you resigned. I had a feeling that it was because of me."

Diane looked straight at him, tears leaving silvery streaks on her cheeks. "The first time I saw you in my penthouse, I really liked you. The last time you were here, I really enjoyed your company. Now I don't know."

"I'm really sorry, Diane. Let's just try to have fun." Dave pleaded. "I don't get a one week suspension that often." Diane half-smiled before she caught herself. She finally nodded in reluctant agreement and Dave's heart grew light.

The rest of the week was spent in candlelight dinners, cliff exploring, trail climbing, bar hopping, and learning how to dance the hula. Dave gave up his room in the suite and they spent every night together, learning how to love and please the other.

Chapter 29

The Test of Trust

Diane pillowed her head on Dave's broad chest. Their conversation was muted, intimate as Dave ran a caressing hand over Diane's smooth back. Diane reached up and kissed him softly on the lips.

"So, do you sleep with all the women you investigate?"

"No. Only 98% of them." Diane made a move to get up in disgust and Dave pulled her back down. "Just kidding! You're the first, honestly."

"Tell me about your love life."

Dave stared at the ceiling. "I had a few girlfriends in high school and college. But nothing clicked seriously. I lived with a woman for about three weeks once. It didn't work out."

"What happened?"

Dave chuckled. "She had seven cats and five dogs all living in the house. I couldn't stand the smell or the constant racket from all those pets."

Diane laughed. "I guess it's my turn now."

"Yep."

"Well, in high school and college I had the usual boyfriends that I went to the movies with and stuff like that. Then in my last year of college I met this boy from Sri Lanka and I liked him a lot. He was kind, quiet, sincere, and loving. Then his family pressured him to come home and marry a Sri Lankan Tamil girl." Diane fell silent for a few seconds. "Then when I started working, I fell in love with a married man. I was attracted to his money, power, and style. We had a lot of fun. Then his needs changed—his wife and kids became important to him. So I dropped him."

Dave took over the line of questions. "What do you love and hate most in life?"

"I love my work." Diane replied without hesitation. "I hate...people who break promises, who are rude, and those who just don't want to be helped."

"I love beautiful girls," Dave squeezed Diane's shoulder playfully, "falling in love and solving difficult cases. I hate people who take advantage of others."

Diane started laughing. "Really, you hate people who take advantage of others? Like when you searched my room and took my safety deposit key when I was out?"

"Hey, I was just doing my job!"

"Doing your job by taking advantage of others." Diane reminded him without malice. "So when it comes to work do your morals and your ethics come in to play or do they conveniently go away?"

"You're right. What I did was wrong, but, as a detective, I had to put my duty first."

"Do you consider that one of your strengths?"

"Not necessarily. My biggest strength is that I never leave a case unsolved."

"Set a goal and achieve it." Diane had a faraway look in her eye. "That's my biggest strength." She propped herself up to be able to see Dave's face. "But surely you have weaknesses also."

Dave smiled. "The one thing I've learned from detective training is never, <u>ever</u> tell anyone your weaknesses. They can be used to literally eat you alive."

"Then I don't have to tell mine, either." Diane said smugly, settling back into Dave's arms.

"You can tell me—I won't take advantage of you."

"Right. So you can eat me alive?

"You still don't trust me?" Diane didn't answer, but the silence was warm in the slight breeze that blew in the window, ruffling the curtains and lifting Diane's hair off the pillow. "I love the breeze…and the sound of the ocean. I only have two more days here, and I'm going to miss this and miss you, Diane."

"So, don't go. Stay here with me."

"I have to go back to my job."

"I have enough to take care of both of us." Diane replied casually.

"Yeah, how much?"

Diane sat up and stared down at Dave. "Are you starting the questions again?"

Dave weighed his decision. "Why don't you tell me that you'll put the jewels back and I'll stop the questions?"

"Tell me, what makes you think I have the jewels?"

"You have the perfect motive. You have access to all the needed keys. You were at Rittman's party. That's your alibi and scapegoat. The Mexican guy you hired to sit in the stairwell for an hour. That's called the diversion. The door alarm that went off to make it look like someone broke in, even though the jewels were taken hours, maybe even days earlier. The truth is, only you would be close enough to Rittman to somehow get the combination to the safe."

Diane studied Dave's face. "What's my motive?"

"No one gives their employees such expensive gifts. Not even Bill Gates. You and Rittman were having an affair. He wanted to have a 'little on the side' and at the same time ensure that you'd never tell. What better way than buying expensive jewels as a 'love bribe.' Diane wrapped the blanket around herself, listening. Dave was on a roll. "Something happened to your relationship and you wanted to punish him or get out. By hiding the jewels you would expose your affair to the world. Pressure from Rittman's important friends, his seeing the pictures of us and then firing you—that's all proof of your relationship."

"What does Paul's party have to do with this?"

"That's called a golden opportunity. What better than being with fifty plus people, including the person you want to get even with, while the robbery is taking place?"

"Okay, so who is this Mexican guy you're talking about?"

"The diversion? The guy hired another man to do the job that you hired him for. The other man admitted he just sat in the stairs leading to the penthouse for 45 minutes. He was only there to help record someone at the building at the time of the crime. He never went up the stairs or into the penthouse—the size seven footprints prove that."

"What about the alarm?"

"You didn't want the alarm to go off when the Mexican guy was supposed to enter the building, but you wanted the alarm sound when he went out—to prove that person took 45 minutes to steal the jewels. You told him to stay that long. A timer must have been connected to the alarm to shut off just before 10:30 pm and come on just after 11:00 pm. You had access to all the keys and, as an architect; you have technical knowledge of how security system works inside as well as outside of a structure and enough knowledge about electrical control systems."

"What about the footprints?"

"The size seven belonged to Peter, the man the Mexican guy hired. The size ten person was never there. You must have put on a pair of size ten shoes and walked from the ground floor to inside your penthouse."

"And the safe? How was that opened?"

"Rittman said that he memorized the combination. Therefore no one could have known the number. The safe is inside your penthouse and you could have easily set up some kind of hidden camera to record the combination."

"Dave, these are pretty good theories. If you're so sure, why don't you arrest me?"

Dave got up and reached for his clothes, smiling. "I'm on suspension right now. But once I get back, maybe."

"What's your proof that I did it?"

"I don't have proof, just a theory. And, Diane, no one's going to arrest you."

"Why not?"

Dave kissed her on the cheek. "I know you're going to put them back. See, if you take the insurance money then you are a thief and you know very well that selling those jewels will be nearly impossible."

"You're good." Diane told him. "You're really good."

Dave gave her a serious look. "Do you need my help to put them back?"

"I told you that I was going to give you a chance to prove that you really came here because you cared about me. Here's that chance. You know that I haven't collected a single cent from the insurance on those jewels, so I haven't done anything technically illegal unless someone can prove that I took them. Which, without my help, you or anyone else never will." Diane pulled on her robe and fastened the tie at her waist. "You were right about my relationship with Paul. He filled six years of my life with empty promises. One day I just fell out of love. So I decided to get out."

"Why did you take the jewels?" Dave was very aware that the case was well on its way to being solved and over.

"It was for protection. Believe me; you don't want to be on the wrong side of Paul. I've known him for six years and I know how he deals with his enemies. If I stopped seeing Paul, he would take everything: the jewels, the penthouse, and my job. I thought about it a long time and came up with a plan." She walked over to the mirror and brushed out her hair. She stared at her reflection, talking as much to it as she was to Dave. "I decided to create a situation to make it known that the jewels were gone. So I had to take the jewels, hide them somewhere, and make it look like a robbery. You actually helped with that."

"How?"

"I watched your interviews about the coin theft and I duplicated some of the events. The glass cutting, the two sets of footprints, the security camera…."

Dave shook his head wryly. "Maybe I should stop with all the interviews in the future."

"I read every newspaper about the coin robbery and then planned the job. After the robbery I got the chance to prove to the world that Paul and I had a relationship because he had bought the jewels and the receipts would show that. He couldn't deny our relationship—that he knew very well. When he told me to look for a new job, I explained my position and my needs. I asked him for the penthouse and the apartment. He didn't have a choice. He also had a lot of cash in the safe—much more than he claimed. I took that too. He would never complain because then a lot of questions would be asked by a lot of people.

"I don't want to take the insurance money and live on the run. The plan doesn't include taking money from the insurance company so it's time to tell them that I found the jewels."

"How are you going to do that?"

"This is where you show I can trust you."

"So where are the jewels?"

"In the safe."

"What? The safe was completely empty! Did you put them back right after we looked around?"

"They've been there the whole time. I made a false bottom in the safe's floor and hid the jewels there. It took me weeks to draft up and make it to match the interior enough to be undetectable."

Dave was suitably impressed. "That's brilliant."

"Now here's the plan: we will leave together to Seattle in two days. The day you go back to work I'll call you and tell you that someone dropped the jewels at my place. You'll inform the insurance company and the case is over. We'll be rich."

"We?"

"Only if you play it right and don't double-cross me. You can't prove I had anything to do with it. But if you do as I say, I can trust my future with you."

Dave stood in deep thought, rubbing a hand along his unshaven chin. "I must be crazy. What am I doing?" Diane stood in front of him and slipped his shirt off his shoulders. "Taking your clothes off." She smiled and leaned in for a kiss, which Dave gladly gave her.

After their passionate love, Dave stood up and started to put on his pants.

"So where did you hide the money?"

" Now don't start that again. You heard enough about the jewels. I am not a fool to tell you where the money is and secondly, no one is going to believe someone took the money and gave it back. So no more questions from you. Now it is my turn to test your trust. Are we clear?"

"Chrystal clear!"

Chapter 30

The Final Test

The flight had arrived on time and now Dave and Diane were standing in the airport parking lot at Dave's car. Planes roared by overhead.

"Diane, I'll take you straight to your penthouse."

"No, you go, and I'll take a cab." Diane set her mouth stubbornly, and Dave rolled his eyes in mock frustration.

"Maybe we should go straight to the station and turn you in." He threatened teasingly.

"Don't joke like that." Diane scolded. "I'll get a cab."

"Fine." Dave threw up his hands in surrender. "I'll see you later."

"I have a few things to do in the morning, please come about noon tomorrow"

"If that is your wish madam, I will be there at noon"

"Okay." Diane smiled and they shared a sweet kiss reminiscent of the day before. She hailed a taxi and hopped in, and was off to her penthouse.

As Diane stepped through the doors of the beautiful building that meant so much to her, she walked over to the security guard Trevor. Trevor got up from his seat with a smile "good evening miss Taylor". "Good evening Trevor. Could you bring my suitcases from the taxi and mail packages from my storage room to penthouse".

"Yes miss Taylor"

Trevor started to walk towards the taxi.

Diane proceeded straight away to the elevator without a second glance.

Diane unlocked the door to her penthouse and the security guard Trevor brought her suitcases, mail, and packages. She sorted through the mail as she wandered towards her bedroom. She finally found what she had been hoping for—a box from Los Angeles. She smelled the box and smiling. She placed the box on her dining table and walked to her bedroom. She noticed a large envelope on her bed with the return address of Rittman Developers on it. She tore it open eagerly and read through the documents carefully. It was all there: the deeds to the penthouse and the Hawaii suite. She smiled triumphantly when her eyes lit on the line that held her name, the line that proclaimed her sole owner of the two properties she loved so dearly.

Diane turned to her closet to hang up her coat. The coat tumbled from her still fingers to the floor. She let out a gasp. Where the safe had sat so sturdily on the shelf was now empty. With trembling fingers, Diane dialed Dave's number.

"Dave, we have a major problem. The safe, it's gone."

"Gone? Are you sure?"

"Yes. I need you, please come now."

"I'm on my way."

Dave strode towards the security guard station, his first stop before Diane's. Security guard Trevor looked understandably nervous at the sight of a stern-looking detective approaching with threatening quickness.

"What day did they remove the safe from Miss Taylor's apartment?" He growled.

Trevor tried to think clearly in his sudden state of panic. "Uh, two, no, three days ago. Maybe two days ago."

"Check your log. I want an exact time. And who came and got it."

"Some storage company. Yep, two days ago exactly." Trevor looked relieved that he could provide at least one right answer.

"What was the company's name?"

"I don't know. Their badges were too small to read." Trevor was starting to look a little defensive at Dave's persistence.

Dave relented a bit and adopted a calmer voice. "The safe weighed a ton and would take forever to get down. Are you telling me that a van sat outside all that time and no one read the name on the side?"

Trevor shrugged. "Sorry. I guess I just never looked."

"Buckley Transport and Storage." Trevor and Dave turned in surprise. An elderly woman hobbled past, leaning heavily on a cane for support. She stopped at the elevators. "I used to live in Buckley about 30 minutes from here. So I remembered the name. I saw it when I went out for my Wednesday afternoon bridge game at 2:00 pm. I saw them moving a big safe. The van was still there when I came back, which was about four."

"Thank you, ma'am." Dave said warmly. The lady nodded and shuffled into the elevator. Dave returned his scathing attention to Trevor and hissed angrily, "A geriatric can do this job better than you." At that moment, Diane appeared from the elevator, stress wrinkling her forehead. Trevor quickly busied himself with something else, hoping Dave was done with him. Dave led Diane into a quiet part of the lobby.

"What's going on?" Diane asked, her voice shaky.

"Rittman had the safe moved to a storage company."

"What are we going to do?"

"I'm going to go over to the storage place tomorrow morning—early—and check to see if it's still there."

"Okay, call me and let me know. Or come by my place, but not until noon or later. I, uh…have something to do in the morning."

"Why did he take the safe?" Dave asked in frustration.

"It's his safe. It wasn't part of our agreement. It was my mistake to forget about it. Maybe he figures he's already lost enough to me."

"Don't worry, I will find the safe and I will come and see you tomorrow about noon"

Dave went straight to his car and Diane went to her penthouse.

Diane sat at her dining table, staring rather happily at the large package on the surface in front of her that Trevor had delivered. It was almost midnight, but she didn't feel tired. She carefully slit open the flaps with a knife and pulled out the contents—a solid bar of milk chocolate. She took it over to the kitchen scale and placed it on top. She was very pleased to see it weighed exactly 26.33 ounces. With a large knife, she hacked off a corner of the chocolate and placed the piece in her mouth. The creamy deliciousness of it was savory beautiful, a work of art. She took a cloth and wiped out the box thoroughly, eating small flakes of chocolate as she did so. Diane then placed the box in a kitchen drawer.

The next morning, Diane walked breezily to the Wells Fargo bank. The cameraman following her and took note of her neck. She was not wearing a necklace. Diane showed her ID to the bank clerk, who escorted her down the long stainless steel corridor and to her safety deposit box where she was left alone. She opened her purse and slipped something from the box and took the necklace she bought a few weeks ago and clasped it around her neck. Diane was ready to go. The cameraman noticing that Diane was wearing the necklace she bought a few weeks ago and taking a photo of Diane as she walked out of the bank. Diane was heading towards her penthouse.

In her penthouse Diane opened the kitchen drawer and pulled out the empty box that had contained the chocolate. She slid something from inside her purse into the box and glanced at the clock—12:03 PM. She put the box back on the table and checked her appearance in a small mirror on the wall. With a deep breath, she went out on the balcony and looked over the railing to see what she had expected to observe. Two police cars were just pulling up, and Dave got out of one of them with two uniformed officers in tow. Diane went back inside and sat on the couch to wait.

Dave reached for the doorbell, but before he could press the button, the door swung open and Diane, pale and serious, stood in front of him. She glanced warily at the two officers with him and Dave took the hint.

"Thank you, officers. I'll take it from here." The cops nodded respectfully and headed back to the elevator. Dave followed Diane into the apartment, where she whirled to face him.

"You scared me! Why the cops?"

Dave pulled a small velvet purse from his pocket. "You don't think I'd travel with over five million dollars worth of jewels unescorted?"

Diane smiled in relief and kissed him long and hard. Dave, laughing, handed over the jewels. He took a seat in a chair and leaned back.

"Do you know what I went through to get the jewels? I went to the storage place at

8:00 AM and they were closed. I waited for one hour for the storage guys to come at 9:00 am to open. Then I had to crawl through lots of furniture and found the safe in a corner. Then I got some help from the storage guys to open the safe and after they left, I opened the hidden bottom and found the jewels. I must be crazy!"

"You're crazy for me. That's why you did it." Diane smiled enigmatically. "Dave, are we ready to call the insurance company?"

"Let's do it. Just don't give him any details. Just tell him that I found the jewels and come ASAP." Dave pulled out his cell phone and Diane took the jewels into the kitchen. With a dramatic flair, she dropped the satchel of jewels directly into the garbage bin. She opened the refrigerator and cut off another hunk off chocolate. When she got back to the living room, Dave had just ended the call. She made herself comfortable on his lap and fed him a morsel of chocolate.

"Insurance guy Mike Sinessi was thrilled and he's on his way." Dave reported when the chocolate piece was gone, smiling hugely. Diane leaned down and covered his mouth with hers.

"This is your reward." After a few minutes, Dave pulled away, eager to tell his tale.

"It was nothing. I found the storage company and just lifted the false bottom with a screw driver."

At that point, Diane didn't really seem to care—she kissed him again, silencing him and any protests he might have had.

Chapter 31

The Surprise

Mike Sinessi, the insurance investigator, knocked sharply on Diane's door. Dave opened the door with a big smile. Mike returned the grin, looking equally as pleased to be able to wrap the case up. He shook Dave's hand. "Let's see what you have." Dave showed Mike into the living room and directed him toward a table. Mike sat and placed his briefcase on the table.

"Well, let's wrap this up." He seemed as enthusiastic as the other two to finish with this case once and for all. Diane handed Mike the chocolate box.

"This box came by mail while I was in Hawaii." She explained. "All the jewels were in it. Don't ask who sent it, because I don't know and don't care." Dave sent Diane a puzzled look, which she returned with a wink. Mike missed every bit of that exchange—he was opening the box carefully. "They're going into a safety deposit box right away." She told him. "I need to get your appraisal papers, take new photos of the jewels, you know for sales arrangements."

"Let's take this one thing at a time. We'll get those to you as soon as possible." Mike replied as he compared the jewels with the current insurance papers. Mike was quiet, looking at every thing carefully. He checked the box where it was mailed from and the cost of the postage. He then pulled a digital scale from his briefcase and proceeded to weigh the box of gems—28.83 ounces. He then weighed them one by one and the total of all those were 26.33 ounces. He jotted down the information and compared it with previously recorded information.

"The weight of the jewels and our records are right on target. There's no sign of tampering with the jewels." Mike checked the postal date. "The cost of the postage corresponds exactly to the weight of the box and the content's. Mike then pulling out photos of the jewels from his bag and checking jewelry with the photos.

"Did you get any money with the box?"

"No, no money just the jewels." Diane answered.

"I thought so. No one is going to return money. Who ever took it knew they can't sell these jewels. These are special, unique jewels and hard to sell. Even if they remove the gems, it will be hard to sell. It was sent back to relieve them of any more stress. Since it came from Los Angeles while you were in Hawaii, I have no problem and I am sure my company will have no problem with it. I am not going to do any more investigation. You know that 60% of the robberies are done by the insurers. I have been in this business for a long time. I know when an insurer steals and tries to cash in on a claim."

"It looks like the case will be moving out of my jurisdiction now," Dave said, without regret.

"I'll talk to Mr. Rittman about the insurance cancellation." Mike replied, getting up from his chair. He reached the door, and then turned back, hesitating. "About those pictures of you two, I instructed one of my photographers to follow you, Miss Taylor, to take photographs of your whereabouts and your movements; we need to have this kind of stuff for the records. It's just part of my job. Also we're required to share those things with the police and with our client. I hope it didn't cause too many problems."

Diane smiled at Dave, and then turned back to Mike. "Some." She admitted. "But it all worked out." Mike nodded thankfully and made his exit.

Dave looked at Diane and picked up the chocolate box. "These are not the jewels that I brought back from the safe. These are pearls, gem stones and diamonds necklaces. The ones I brought back were mostly white like diamonds and a few red color stones. No pearls or real expensive looking necklaces".

Diane's face became serious as she pointing her fingers at the jewels explained. "These are rubies, emeralds, and sapphires. They are real—they are the jewels that were stolen".

"Then where are the ones that I brought back from the safe?"

"In the kitchen garbage bin. They are just cosmetic jewels."

Dave was getting a little angry. "So, I went there for nothing?"

"Don't say it was for nothing. You've proved that you care about me and I can trust you."

"That wasn't a fair thing to do." Dave protested.

Diane's look grew hard. "Okay, define 'fair.' I let you stay in my place; you went into my room and imprinted my bank deposit key when I was away. Who's talking about fair? I did it this way to get even. I gave you a chance to prove that you cared about me and you showed it."

"Why would you go that far for proof?"

"To make sure that I can trust you and achieve my goal." Diane smiled.

"What goal?"

"That's for you to find out."

"Another puzzle?"

Diane shrugged. "You're good at solving puzzles, remember?"

"Tell me one thing: where did you really hide the jewels?' Dave was very curious about that.

"They were hidden in the safe's false bottom until I returned from Hawaii the last time. With your clever idea of copying my safety deposit key, I knew that you had already checked my safety deposit box at the bank. After I had the fight with Paul, I took the jewels from the safe and put them in my bank safety deposit box because I suspected Paul might take the safe. Since you had already checked my bank safety deposit box, I figured that you wouldn't check it again. I took a chance. Sometimes in life you have to take chances to reach your goals. This morning I went to the bank and took them."

"What about the box with the right weight and correct stamps?"

"I asked a friend of mine in Los Angeles to send me exactly 26.33 ounces of chocolate—that's how much the jewels weighed. The beauty with chocolate is, you can cut it to any weight you want or need. Then the box would stay the same weight even when I put the jewels in it."

"So I lost my case this time?"

Diane slid into his arms. "No, you won the case and she's yours. You won her heart and a luxury life on a faraway island. But, that's only if you want it." She raised her eyebrows, waiting for his answer.

"First I have to go tell my boss to shove this job up his you-know-where."

Diane laughed long and loud.

The Hawaiian mid-morning sun beat down upon Dave and Diane as they sat in matching beach chairs, their feet buried in piles of hot sand. The waves lapped at their feet and seagulls cried overhead. They were holding hands—they were doing that a lot these days.

"I was just thinking." Dave said suddenly. "What happens if you want to get rid of me?"

"What are you talking about?" Diane asked with a laugh.

"Well, you got rid of Rittman."

"You're definitely *not* Paul."

"That's right. I'm a detective. I mean, an *ex*-detective. You're going to have to be a lot more deceptive and cunning with me than you were with Paul Rittman."

Diane smiled at him cheekily. "I've already thought it out."

"Really?"

"Yes, to the very last detail."

"You've already thought that far ahead?" Now Dave was getting worried.

"Yup. And it's really quite simple."

"Simple, huh? Give me a clue."

"All I need are seven cats and five dogs." Dave grabbed her, punishing her with kisses as she shrieked with laughter. He finally let her up.

"So you're done with your goals, right?" He asked, half-jokingly.

"No, two more left."

"Two more?"

Diane smiled. "A diamond ring on my left finger and a baby in my tummy."

"Oh no, I shouldn't have asked."